The Hashish Man
and other stories

The Hashish Man

and other stories

by

Lord Dunsany

Manic D Press
San Francisco

Published by Manic D Press. For more information, contact Manic D Press, P.O. Box 410804, San Francisco, California 94141.

Editor: Jon Longhi
Thanks to Carson Hall for his assistance
Cover design: Brian Walls / e Conspiracy

5 4 3 2

Library of Congress Cataloging-in-Publication Data

Dunsany, Edward John Moreton Drax Plunkett, Baron, 1878-1957.
The hashish man & other stories / by Lord Dunsany.
p. cm.
ISBN 0-916397-45-9 (pbk.)
1. Fantastic fiction, English--Irish authors. I. Title.
II. Title: Hashish man and other stories.
PR6007.U6H3 1996
823'.912--dc21 96-45809
CIP

Distributed to the trade by Publishers Group West

Contents

Introduction

Literature is the best form of time travel. You can visit any era in books. For years the world has seemed insane and falling apart. Every day, the newspapers are filled with chaos, ruin, and despair. The future often seems a broken impossible dream. One of the few things that has assuaged my fear and paranoia has been reading literature from the past, and realizing civilization has remained essentially unchanged since its beginnings. Human nature has been the same since before the time of Homer when the literary record crumbles apart in ancient Sumerian clay tablets.

This time travel through books has led to amazing discoveries of lost geniuses buried beneath the sands of passing decades. After reading certain authors, I would continue farther back and read works by the writers who had inspired them. In many cases, the muses were as good, if not better, than their derivatives. It was this process that led me to Lord Dunsany.

I found Dunsany through H. P. Lovecraft. The *Weird Tales* writer often cited the Irish baron as a writer who had had a great effect on him. It is well that Lovecraft paid homage to him, because certain elements of Lovecraft's style are obviously borrowed from the Irishman. The whole theme of traveling to other worlds while under the influence of dreams had been fully expressed by Dunsany by the time Lovecraft began his writing career. So too had the themes of crumbling cities lost in the sands of time, and faded civilizations that could occasionally strike back at the living through ancient prophecies and curses. In the case of these crumbling necropolises, all modern science fiction writers owe a tremendous percentage of their literary output to raw materials earlier mined by Dunsany.

Unlike Lovecraft, Lord Dunsany is less a horror writer than a composer of weird fantasy and magical realism. He lacks the throbbing phantasmagorical revulsion of Lovecraft and instead replaces it with dreamlike wonder. His voice flows with a lush style full of vivid colorful details reminiscent of the nuances in a Maxfield Parrish painting. At times these details veer toward the noisome realm of elves and hobbits, but at his best, the stories launch into a psychedelic rave-up of language and imagery. Stories like *Idle Days On The Yann* meander gracefully, and it's great fun riding the hallucinations. At other times, Dunsany pens a mean little ghost story that goes straight for the jugular.

Besides his effect on the *Weird Tales* writers, other science fiction and fantasy writers have popularized many of his themes: heroic quests that have no ending and eventually just peter out in old age, chaos, and madness; huge civilizations that disappear overnight thanks to the malicious agency of some unseen presence. His knights rode through the comics of Jack Kirby, and his sultans leered from the pulp magazines of the '30s. In *A Story of Land and Sea*, Captain Shard pilots a boat which sails across the desert on huge wheels, just like the main vehicle in the movie *Time Bandits.*

The power of great writing goes beyond the printed page and becomes a part of the world's cultural consciousness. It is a profound pleasure to introduce these remarkable stories, which originally appeared in *A Dreamer's Tales* (1910), *Fifty-One Tales* (1915), and *Tales of Wonder* (1916). After reading the stories of Lord Dunsany, it becomes clear that his works have been reborn as strange changelings in the creations of those he has inspired, reincarnation in the beasts of our collective imagination.

Jon Longhi
San Francisco

Charon

Charon leaned forward and rowed. All things were one with his weariness.

It was not with him a matter of years or of centuries, but of wide floods of time, and an old heaviness and a pain in the arms that had become for him part of the scheme that the gods had made and was of a piece with Eternity.

If the gods had even sent him a contrary wind it would have divided all time in his memory into two equal slabs.

So grey were all things always where he was that if any radiance lingered a moment among the dead, on the face of such a queen perhaps as Cleopatra, his eyes could not have perceived it.

It was strange that the dead nowadays were coming in such numbers. They were coming in thousands where they used to come in fifties. It was neither Charon's duty nor his wont to ponder in his grey soul why these things might be. Charon leaned forward and rowed.

Then no one came for a while. It was not unusual for the gods to send no one down from Earth for such a space. But the gods knew best.

Then one man came alone. And the little shade sat shivering on a lonely bench and the great boat pushed off. Only one passenger; the gods knew best.

And great and weary Charon rowed on and on beside the little, silent, shivering ghost.

And the sound of the river was like a mighty sigh that Grief in the beginning had sighed among her sisters, and that could not die like the echoes of human sorrow failing on earthly hills, but was as old as time and the pain in Charon's arms.

Then the boat from the slow, grey river loomed up to the coast of Dis and the little, silent shade still shivering stepped ashore, and Charon turned the boat to go wearily back to the world. Then the little shadow spoke, that had been a man.

"I am the last," he said.

No one had ever made Charon smile before, no one before had ever made him weep.

The Three Infernal Jokes

This is the story that the desolate man told to me on the lonely Highland road one autumn evening with winter coming on and the stags roaring.

The saddening twilight, the mountain already black, the dreadful melancholy of the stags' voices, his friendless mournful face, all seemed to be of some most sorrowful play staged in that valley by an outcast god, a lonely play of which the hills were part and he only the actor.

For long we watched each other drawing out of the solitudes of those forsaken spaces. Then when we met he spoke.

"I will tell you a thing that will make you die of laughter. I will keep it to myself no longer. But first I must tell you how I came by it."

I do not give the story in his words with all his woeful interjections and the misery of his frantic self-reproaches for I would not convey unnecessarily to my readers that atmosphere of sadness that was about all he said and that seemed to go with him wherever he moved.

It seemed that he had been a member of a club, a West-end club he called it, a respectable but quite inferior affair, probably in the City: agents belonged to it, fire insurance mostly, but life insurance and motor-agents too, it was in fact a touts' club.

It seems that a few of them one evening, forgetting for a moment their encyclopaedias and non-stop tyres, were talking loudly over a card-table when the game had ended about their personal virtues, and a very little man with waxed moustaches who disliked the taste of wine was boasting heartily of his temperance. It was then that he who told this mournful story, drawn on by the boasts of others, leaned forward a little over the green blaze into the light of the two guttering candles and revealed, no doubt a little shyly, his own extraordinary virtue. One woman to him was as ugly as another.

And the silenced boasters arose and went home to bed leaving him all alone, as he supposed, with his unequalled virtue. And yet he was not alone, for when the rest had gone there arose a member out of a deep arm-chair at the dark end of the room and walked across to him, a man whose occupation he did not know and only now suspects.

"You have," said the stranger, "a surpassing virtue."

"I have no possible use for it," my poor friend replied.

"Then doubtless you would sell it cheap," said the stranger.

Something in the man's manner or appearance made the desolate teller of this mournful tale feel his own inferiority, which probably made him feel acutely shy, so that his mind abased itself as an Oriental does his body in the presence of a superior, or perhaps he was sleepy, or merely a little drunk. Whatever it was he only mumbled "O yes," instead of contradicting so mad a remark. And the stranger led the way to the room where the telephone was.

"I think you will find my firm will give a good price for it," he said: and without more ado he began with a pair of pincers to cut the wire of the telephone and the receiver. The old waiter who looked after the club they had left shuffling round the other room putting things away for the night.

"Whatever are you doing of?" said my friend.

"This way," said the stranger. Along a passage they went and away to the back of the club and there the stranger leaned out of a window and fastened the severed wires to the lightning conductor. My friend has no doubt of that, a broad ribbon of copper, half an inch wide, perhaps wider, running down from the roof to the earth.

"Hell," said the stranger with his mouth to the telephone; then silence for a while with his ear to the receiver, leaning out of the window. And then my friend heard his poor virtue being several times repeated, and then words like yes and No.

"They offer you three jokes," said the stranger, "which shall make all who hear them simply die of laughter."

I think my friend was reluctant then to have anything more to do with it, he wanted to go home; he said he didn't want any jokes.

"They think very highly of your virtue," said the stranger. And at that, odd as it seems, my friend wavered, for logically if they thought highly of the goods they should have paid a higher price.

"O all right," he said.

The extraordinary document that the agent drew from his pocket ran something like this:

"I ..... in consideration of three new jokes received from Mr. Montagu-Montague, hereinafter to be called the agent, and warranted to be as by him stated and described, do assign to him, yield, abrogate, and give up all recognitions, emoluments, perquisites or rewards due to me Here or Elsewhere on account of the following virtue, to wit and that is to say ..... that all women are to me equally ugly." The last eight words were being filled in in ink by Mr. Montagu-Montague.

My poor friend duly signed it. "These are the jokes," said the agent. They were boldly written on three slips of paper. "They don't seem very funny," said the other when he had read them. "You are immune," said Montagu-Montague, "but anyone else who hears them will simply die of laughter: that we guarantee."

An American firm had bought at the price of waste paper a hundred thousand copies of The Dictionary of Electricity written when electricity was new, — and it had turned out that even then its author had not rightly grasped his subject, — the firm had paid 10,000 pounds to a respectable English paper (no other in fact than the Briton) for the use of its name, and to obtain orders for The Briton Dictionary of Electricity was the occupation of my unfortunate friend. He seems to have had a way with him. Apparently he knew by a glance at a man, or a look round at his garden, whether to recommend the book as "an absolutely up-to-date achievement, the finest thing of its kind in the world of modern science" or as "at once quaint and imperfect, a thing to buy and to keep as a tribute to those dear old times that are gone." So he went on with this quaint though usual business, putting aside the memory of that night as an occasion on which he had "somewhat exceeded" as they say in circles where a spade is called neither a spade nor an agricultural implement but is never mentioned at all, being altogether too vulgar.

And then one night he put on his suit of dress clothes and found the three jokes in the pocket. That was perhaps a shock. He seems to have thought it over carefully then, and the end of it was he gave a dinner at the club to twenty of the members. The dinner would do no harm he thought -might even help the business, and if the joke came off he would be a witty fellow, and two jokes still up his sleeve.

Whom he invited or how the dinner went I do not know for he began to speak rapidly and came straight to the point, as a stick that nears a cataract suddenly goes faster and faster. The dinner was duly served, the port went round, the twenty men were smoking, two waiters loitered, when he after carefully reading the best of the jokes told it down the table. They laughed. One man accidentally inhaled his cigar smoke and spluttered, the two waiters overheard and tittered behind their hands, one man, a bit of a raconteur himself, quite clearly wished not to laugh, but his veins swelled dangerously in trying to keep it back, and in the end he laughed too. The joke had succeeded; my friend smiled at the thought; he wished to say little deprecating things to the man on his right; but the laughter did not stop and the waiters would not be silent. He waited, and waited wondering; the laughter went roaring on, distinctly louder now, and the waiters as loud as any. It had gone on for three or four minutes when this frightful thought leaped up all at once in his mind: *it was forced laughter!* However could anything have induced him to tell so foolish a joke? He saw its absurdity as in revelation; and the more he thought of it as these people laughed at him, even the waiters too, the more he felt that he could never lift up his head with his brother touts again. And still the laughter went roaring and choking on. He was very angry. There was not much use in having a friend, he thought, if one silly joke could not be overlooked; he had fed them too. And then he felt that he had no friends at all, and his anger faded away, and a great unhappiness came down on him, and he got quietly up and slunk from the room and slipped away from the club. Poor man, he scarcely had the heart next morning even to glance at the papers, but you did not need to glance at them, big type was bandied about that day as though it were common type, the words of the headlines stared at you; and the headlines said: Twenty-Two Men Dead at a Club.

Yes, he saw it then: the laughter had not stopped, some had probably burst blood vessels, some must have choked, some succumbed to nausea, heart-failure must have mercifully taken some, and they were his friends after all, and none had escaped, not even the waiters. It was that infernal joke.

He thought out swiftly, and remembers clear as a nightmare, the drive to Victoria Station, the boat-train to Dover and going disguised to the boat: and on the boat pleasantly smiling, almost obsequious, two constables that wished to speak for a moment with Mr. Watkyn-Jones. That was his name.

In a third-class carriage with handcuffs on his wrists, with forced conversation when any, he returned between his captors to be tried for murder at the High Court of Bow.

At the trial he was defended by a young barrister of considerable ability who had gone into the cabinet in order to enhance his forensic reputation. And he was ably defended. It is no exaggeration to say that the speech for the defence showed it to be usual, even natural and right, to give a dinner to twenty men and to slip away without ever saying a word, leaving all, with the waiters, dead.

That was the impression left in the minds of the jury. And Mr. Watkyn-Jones felt himself practically free, with all the advantages of his awful experience, and his two jokes intact. But lawyers are still experimenting with the new act which allows a prisoner to give evidence. They do not like to make no use of it for fear they may be thought not to know of the act, and a lawyer who is not in touch with the very latest laws is soon regarded as not being up to date and he may drop as much as 50,000 pounds a year in fees. And therefore though it always hangs their clients they hardly like to neglect it.

Mr. Watkyn-Jones was put in the witness box. There he told the simple truth, and a very poor affair it seemed after the impassioned and beautiful things that were uttered by the counsel for the defence. Men and women had wept when they heard that. They did not weep when they heard Watkyn-Jones. Some tittered. It no longer seemed a right and natural thing to leave one's guests all dead and to fly the country. Where was Justice, they asked, if anyone could do that? And when his story was told the judge rather happily asked if he could make him die of laughter too. And what was the joke? For in so grave a place as a Court of Justice no fatal effects need be feared. And hesitatingly the prisoner pulled from his pocket the three slips of paper: and perceived for the first time that the one on which the first and best joke had been written had become quite blank. Yet he could remember it, and only too clearly. And he told it from memory to the Court.

"An Irishman once on being asked by his master to buy a morning paper said in his usual witty way, 'Arrah and begorrah and I will be after wishing you the top of the morning.'"

No joke sounds quite so good the second time it is told, it seems to lose something of its essence, but Watkyn-Jones was not prepared for the awful stillness with which this one was received; nobody smiled; and it had killed twenty-two men. The joke was bad, devilish bad; counsel for the defence was frowning, and an usher was looking in a little bag for something the judge wanted. And at this moment, as though from far away, without his wishing it, there entered into the prisoner's head, and shone there and would not go, this old bad proverb: "As well be hung for a sheep as for a lamb." The jury seemed just about to retire. "I have another joke," said Watkyn-Jones, and then and there he read from the second slip of paper. He watched the paper curiously to see if it would go blank, occupying his mind with so slight a thing as men in dire distress very often do, and the words were almost immediately expunged, swept swiftly as if by a hand, and he saw the paper before him as blank as the first. And they were laughing this time, judge, jury, counsel for the prosecution, audience and all, and the grim men that watched him upon either side. There was no mistake about this joke.

He did not stay to see the end, and walked out with his eyes fixed on the ground, unable to bear a glance to the right or left. And since then he has wandered, avoiding ports and roaming lonely places. Two years have known him on the Highland roads, often hungry, always friendless, always changing his district, wandering lonely on with his deadly joke.

Sometimes for a moment he will enter inns, driven by cold and hunger, and hear men in the evening telling jokes and even challenging him; but he sits desolate and silent, lest his only weapon should escape from him and his last joke spread mourning in a hundred cots. His beard has grown and turned grey and is mixed with moss and weeds, so that no one, I think, not even the police, would recognise him now for that tout that sold The Briton Dictionary of Electricity in such a different land.

He paused, his story told, and then his lip quivered as though he would say more, and I believe he intended then and there to yield up his deadly joke on that Highland road and to go forth then with his three blank slips of paper, perhaps to a felon's cell, with one more murder added to his crimes, but harmless at last to man. I therefore hurried on, and only heard him mumbling sadly behind me, standing bowed and broken, all alone in the twilight, perhaps telling over and over even then the last infernal joke.

The Guest

A young man came into an ornate restaurant at eight o'clock in London.

He was alone, but two places had been laid at the table which was reserved for him. He had chosen the dinner very carefully, by letter a week before.

A waiter asked him about the other guest.

"You probably won't see him till the coffee comes," the young man told him; so he was served alone.

Those at adjacent tables might have noticed the young man continually addressing the empty chair and carrying on a monologue with it throughout his elaborate dinner.

"I think you knew my father," he said to it over the soup. "I sent for you this evening," he continued, "because I want you to do me a good turn; in fact I must insist on it."

There was nothing eccentric about the man except for this habit of addressing an empty chair, certainly he was eating as good a dinner as any sane man could wish for.

After the Burgundy had been served he became more voluble in his monologue, not that he spoiled his wine by drinking excessively.

"We have several acquaintances in common," he said. "I met King Seti a year ago in Thebes. I think he has altered very little since you knew him. I thought his forehead a little low for a king's. Cheops has left the house that he built for your reception, he must have prepared for you years and years. I suppose you have seldom been entertained like that. I ordered this dinner over a week ago. I thought then that a lady might come with me, but as she wouldn't I've asked you. She may not after all be as lovely as Helen of Troy. Was Helen very lovely? Not when you knew her, perhaps. You were lucky in Cleopatra, you must have known her when she was in her prime.

"You never knew the mermaids nor the fairies nor the lovely goddesses of long ago, that's where we have the best of you."

He was silent when the waiters came to his table, but rambled merrily on as soon as they left, still turned to the empty chair.

"You know I saw you here in London only the other day. You were on a motor bus going down Ludgate Hill. It was going much too fast. London is a good place. But I shall be glad enough to leave it. It was in London that I met the lady I that was speaking about. If it hadn't been for London I probably shouldn't have met her, and if it hadn't been for London she probably wouldn't have had so much besides me to amuse her. It cuts both ways."

He paused once to order coffee, gazing earnestly at the waiter and putting a sovereign in his hand. "Don't let it be chicory," said he.

The waiter brought the coffee, and the young man dropped a tabloid of some sort into his cup.

"I don't suppose you come here very often," he went on. "Well, you probably want to be going. I haven't taken you much out of your way, there is plenty for you to do in London."

Then having drunk his coffee he fell on the floor by a foot of the empty chair, and a doctor who was dining in the room bent over him and announced to the anxious manager the visible presence of the young man's guest.

Thirteen at Table

In front of a spacious fireplace of the old kind, when the logs were well alight, and men with pipes and glasses were gathered before it in great easeful chairs, and the wild weather outside and the comfort that was within, and the season of the year — for it was Christmas — and the hour of the night, all called for the weird or uncanny, then out spoke the ex-master of foxhounds and told this tale.

I once had an odd experience too. It was when I had the Bromley and Sydenham, the year I gave them up — as a matter of fact it was the last day of the season. It was no use going on because there were no foxes left in the county, and London was sweeping down on us. You could see it from the kennels all along the skyline like a terrible army in grey, and masses of villas every year came skirmishing down our valleys. Our coverts were mostly on the hills, and as the town came down upon the valleys the foxes used to leave them and go right away out of the county and they never returned. I think they went by night and moved great distances. Well it was early April and we had drawn blank all day, and at the last draw of all, the very last of the season, we found a fox. He left the covert with his back to London and its railways and villas and wire and slipped away towards the chalk country and open Kent. I felt as I once felt as a child on one summer's day when I found a door in a garden where I played luckily left ajar, and I pushed it open and the wide lands were before me and waving fields of corn.

We settled down into a steady gallop and the fields began to drift by under us, and a great wind arose full of fresh breath. We left the clay lands where the bracken grows and came to a valley at the edge of the chalk. As we went down into it we saw the fox go up the other side like a shadow that crosses the evening, and glide into a wood that stood on the top. We saw a flash of primroses in the wood and we were out the other side, hounds hunting perfectly and the fox still going absolutely straight. It began to dawn on me then that we were in for a great hunt, I took a deep breath when I thought of it; the taste of the air of that perfect Spring afternoon as it came to one galloping, and the thought of a great run, were together like some old rare wine. Our faces now were to another valley, large fields led down to it, with easy hedges, at the bottom of it a bright blue stream went singing and a rambling village smoked, the sunlight on the opposite slopes danced like a fairy; and all along the top old woods were frowning, but they dreamed of Spring. The "field" had fallen off and were far behind and my only human companion was James, my old first whip, who had a hound's instinct, and a personal animosity against a fox that even embittered his speech.

Across the valley the fox went as straight as a railwayline, and again we went without a check straight through the woods at the top. I remember hearing men sing or shout as they walked home from work, and sometimes children whistled; the sounds came up from the village to the woods at the top of the valley. After that we saw no more villages, but valley after valley arose and fell before us as though we were voyaging some strange and stormy sea, and all the way before us the fox went dead upwind like the fabulous Flying Dutchman. There was no one in sight now but my first whip and me, we had both of us got on to our second horses as we drew the last covert.

Two or three times we checked in those great lonely valleys beyond the village, but I began to have inspirations, I felt a strange certainty within me that this fox was going on straight up-wind till he died or until night came and we could hunt no longer, so I reversed the ordinary methods and only cast straight ahead and always we picked up the scent again at once. I believe that this fox was the last one left in the villa-haunted lands and that he was prepared to leave them for remote uplands far from men, that if we had come the following day he would not have been there, and that we just happened to hit off his journey.

Evening began to descend upon the valleys, still the hounds drifted on, like the lazy but unresting shadows of clouds upon a summer's day, we saw two maidens move towards a hidden farm, one of them singing softly; no other sounds, but ours, disturbed the leisure and the loneliness of haunts that seemed not yet to have known the inventions of steam and gun-powder (even as China, they say, in some of her furthest mountains does not yet know that she has fought Japan.).

And now the day and our horses were wearing out, but that resolute fox held on. I began to work out the run and wonder where we were. The last landmark I had ever seen before must have been over five miles back and from there to the start was at least ten miles more. If only we could kill! Then the sun set. I wondered what chance we had of killing our fox. I looked at James' face as he rode beside me. He did not seem to have lost any confidence, yet his horse was as tired as mine. It was a good clear twilight and the scent was as strong as ever, and the fences were easy enough, but those valleys were terribly trying and they still rolled on and on. It looked as if the light would outlast all possible endurance both of the fox and the horses, if the scent held good and he did not go to ground, otherwise night would end it. For long we had seen no houses and no roads, only chalk slopes with the twilight on them, and here and there some sheep, and scattered copses darkening in the evening. At some moment I seemed to realize all at once that the light was spent and that darkness was hovering, I looked at James, he was solemnly shaking his head. Suddenly in a little wooded valley we saw climb over the oaks the red-brown gables of a queer old house, at that instant I saw the fox scarcely heading by fifty yards. We blundered through a wood in full sight of the house, but no avenue led up to it or even a path nor were there any signs of wheel-marks anywhere. Already lights shone here and there in windows. We were in a park, and a fine park, but unkempt beyond credibility; brambles grew everywhere. It was too dark to see the fox any more but we knew that he was dead beat, the hounds were just before us, — and a four-foot railing of oak. I shouldn't have tried it on a fresh horse at the beginning of a run, and here was a horse near his last gasp. But what a run! an event standing out in a lifetime, and the hounds close up on their fox, slipping into the darkness as I hesitated. I decided to try it. My horse rose about eight inches and took it fair with his breast, and the oak log flew into handfuls of wet decay — it was rotten with years. And then we were on a lawn and at the far end of it the hounds were tumbling over their fox. Fox, horses and light were all done together at the end of a twenty-mile point. We made some noise then, but nobody came out of the queer old house. I felt pretty stiff as I walked round to the hall door with the mask and the brush while James went with the hounds and the two horses to look for the stables. I rang a bell marvelously encrusted with rust, and after a long while the door opened a little way revealing a hall with much old armour in it and the shabbiest butler that I have ever known.

I asked him who lived there. Sir Richard Arlen. I explained that my horse could go no further that night and that I wished to ask Sir Richard Arlen for a bed for the night.

"O, no one ever comes here, sir," said the butler.

I pointed out that I had come.

"I don't think it would be possible, sir," he said. This annoyed me and I asked to see Sir Richard, and insisted until he came. Then I apologised and explained the situation. He looked only fifty, but a Varsity oar on the wall with the date of the early seventies, made him older than that; his face had something of the shy look of the hermit; he regretted that he had not room to put me up. I was sure that this was untrue, also I had to be put up there, there was nowhere else within miles, so I almost insisted.

Then to my astonishment he turned to the butler and they talked it over in an undertone. At last they seemed to think that they could manage it, though clearly with reluctance. It was by now seven o'clock and Sir Richard told me he dined at half past seven. There was no question of clothes for me other than those I stood in, as my host was shorter and broader. He showed me presently to the drawing-room and there he reappeared before half past seven in evening dress and a white waistcoat. The drawing-room was large and contained old furniture but it was rather worn than venerable, an Aubusson carpet flapped about the floor, the wind seemed momentarily to enter the room, and old draughts haunted corners; the stealthy feet of rats that were never at rest indicated the extent of the ruin that time had wrought in the wainscot; somewhere far off a shutter flapped to and fro, the guttering candles were insufficient to light so large a room. The gloom that these things suggested was quite in keeping with Sir Richard's first remark to me after he entered the room: "I must tell you, sir, that I have led a wicked life. O, a very wicked life."

Such confidences from a man much older than oneself after one has known him for half an hour are so rare that any possible answer merely does not suggest itself. I said rather slowly, "O, really," and chiefly to forestall another such remark I said, "What a charming house you have."

"Yes," he said, "I have not left it for nearly forty years. Since I left the Varsity. One is young there, you know, and one has opportunities; but I make no excuses, no excuses." And the door slipping in its rusty latch, came drifting on the draught into the room, and the long carpet flapped and the hangings upon the walls, then the draught fell rustling away and the door slammed to again.

"Ah, Marianne," he said, "we have a guest to-night. Mr. Linton. This is Marianne Gib." And everything became clear to me. "Mad," I said to myself, for no one had entered the room.

The rats ran up the length of the room behind the wainscotting ceaselessly, and the wind unlatched the door again and the folds of the carpet fluttered up to our feet and stopped there, for our weight held it down.

"Let me introduce Mr. Linton," said my host — "Lady Mary Errinjer."

The door slammed back again. I bowed politely. Even had I been invited I should have humoured him, but it was the very least that an uninvited guest could do.

This kind of thing happened eleven times, the rustling, and the fluttering of the carpet, and the footsteps of the rats, and the restless door, and then the sad voice of my host introducing me to phantoms. Then for some while we waited while I struggled with the situation; conversation flowed slowly. And again the draught came trailing up the room, while the flaring candles filled it with hurrying shadows. "Ah, late again, Cicely," said my host in his soft, mournful way. "Always late, Cicely." Then I went down to dinner with that man and his mind and the twelve phantoms that haunted it. I found a long table with fine old silver on it and places laid for fourteen. The butler was now in evening dress, there were fewer draughts in the dining-room, the scene was less gloomy there. "Will you sit next to Rosalind at the other end," Sir Richard said to me. "She always takes the head of the table, I wronged her most of all."

I said, "I shall be delighted."

I looked at the butler closely, but never did I see by any expression of his face or by anything that he did any suggestion that he waited upon less than fourteen people in the complete possession of all their faculties. Perhaps a dish appeared to be refused more often than taken but every glass was equally filled with champagne. At first I found little to say, but when Sir Richard speaking from the far end of the table said, "You are tired, Mr. Linton," I was reminded that I owed something to a host upon whom I had forced myself. It was excellent champagne and with the help of a second glass I made the effort to begin a conversation with Miss Helen Errold for whom the place upon one side of me was laid. It came more easily to me very soon, I frequently paused in my monologue, like Mark Antony, for a reply, and sometimes I turned and spoke to Miss Rosalind Smith. Sir Richard at the other end talked sorrowfully on, he spoke as a condemned man might speak to his judge, and yet somewhat as a judge might speak to one that he has condemned wrongly. My own mind began to turn to mournful things. I drank another glass of champagne, but I was still thirsty. I felt as if all the moisture in my body had been blown away over the downs of Kent by the wind up which we had galloped. Still I was not talking enough; my host was looking at me. I made another effort, after all I had something to talk about, a twenty-mile point is not often seen in a lifetime, especially south of the Thames. I began to describe the run to Rosalind Smith. I could see then that my host was pleased, the sad look in his face gave a kind of flicker, like mist upon the mountains on a miserable day when a faint puff comes from the sea and the mist would lift if it could. And the butler refilled my glass very attentively. I asked her first if she hunted, and paused and began my story. I told her where we had found the fox and how fast and straight he had gone, and how I had got through the village by keeping to the road, while the little gardens and wire, and then the river, had stopped the rest of the field. I told her the kind of country that we crossed and how splendid it looked in Spring, and how mysterious the twilight came, and what a glorious horse I had and how wonderfully he went. I was so fearfully thirsty after the great hunt that I had to stop for a moment now and then, but I went on with my description of that famous run, for I had warmed to the subject, and after all there was nobody to tell of it but me except my old whipper-in, and "the old fellow's probably drunk by now," I thought. I described to her minutely the exact spot in the run at which it had come to me clearly that this was going to be the greatest hunt in the whole history of Kent. Sometimes I forgot incidents that had happened as one well may in a run of twenty miles, and then I had to fill in the gaps by inventing. I was pleased to be able to make the party go off well by means of my conversation, and besides that the lady to whom I was speaking was extremely pretty: I do not mean in a flesh and blood kind of way but there were little shadowy lines about the chair beside me that hinted at an unusually graceful figure when Miss Rosalind Smith was alive; and I began to perceive that what I first mistook for the smoke of guttering candles and a table-cloth waving in the draught was in reality an extremely animated company who listened, and not without interest, to my story of by far the greatest hunt that the world had ever known: indeed I told them that I would confidently go further and predict that never in the history of the world would there be such a run again. Only my throat was terribly dry. And then as it seemed they wanted to hear more about my horse. I had forgotten that I had come there on a horse, but when they reminded me it all came back; they looked so charming leaning over the table intent upon what I said, that I told them everything they wanted to know. Everything was going so pleasantly if only Sir Richard would cheer up. I heard his mournful voice now and then — these were very pleasant people if only he would take them the right way. I could understand that he regretted the past, but the early seventies seemed centuries away and I felt sure that he misunderstood these ladies, they were not so revengeful as he seemed to suppose. I wanted to show him how cheerful they really were, and so I made a joke and they all laughed at it, and then I chaffed them a bit, especially Rosalind, and nobody resented it in the very least. And still Sir Richard sat there with that unhappy look, like one that has ended weeping because it is vain and has not the consolation even of tears.

We had been a long time there and many of the candles had burned out, but there was light enough. I was glad to have an audience for my exploit, and being happy myself I was determined Sir Richard should be. I made more jokes and they still laughed good-naturedly; some of the jokes were a little broad perhaps but no harm was meant. And then — I do not wish to excuse myself — but I had had a harder day than I ever had had before and without knowing it I must have been completely exhausted; in this state the champagne had found me, and what would have been harmless at any other time must have somehow got the better of me when quite tired out — anyhow I went too far, I made some joke — I cannot in the least remember what — that suddenly seemed to offend them. I felt all at once a commotion in the air, I looked up and saw that they had all arisen from the table and were sweeping towards the door: I had not time to open it but it blew open on a wind, I could scarcely see what Sir Richard was doing because only two candles were left, I think the rest blew out when the ladies suddenly rose. I sprang up to apologise, to assure them

— and then fatigue overcame me as it had overcome my horse at the last fence, I clutched at the table but the cloth came away and then I fell. The fall, and the darkness on the floor and the pent up fatigue of the day overcame me all three together.

The sun shone over glittering fields and in at a bedroom window and thousands of birds were chanting to the Spring, and there I was in an old four-poster bed in a quaint old panelled bedroom, fully dressed and wearing long muddy boots; someone had taken my spurs and that was all. For a moment I failed to realize and then it all came back, my enormity and the pressing need of an abject apology to Sir Richard. I pulled an embroidered bell rope until the butler came. He came in perfectly cheerful and indescribably shabby. I asked him if Sir Richard was up, and he said he had just gone down, and told me to my amazement that it was twelve o'clock. I asked to be shown in to Sir Richard at once. He was in his smoking-room.

"Good morning," he said cheerfully the moment I went in. I went directly to the matter in hand.

"I fear that I insulted some ladies in your house —" I began.

"You did indeed," he said, "You did indeed." And then he burst into tears and took me by the hand. "How can I ever thank you?" he said to me then. "We have been thirteen at table for thirty years and I never dared to insult them because I had wronged them all, and now you have done it and I know they will never dine here again." And for a long time he still held my hand, and then he gave it a grip and a kind of shake which I took to mean "Goodbye" and I drew my hand away then and left the house. And I found James in the stables with the hounds and asked him how he had fared, and James, who is a man of very few words, said he could not rightly remember, and I got my spurs from the butler and climbed on to my horse and slowly we rode away from that queer old house, and slowly we wended home, for the hounds were footsore but happy and the horses were tired still. And when we recalled that the hunting season was ended we turned our faces to Spring and thought of the new things that try to replace the old. And that very year I heard, and have often heard since, of dances and happier dinners at Sir Richard Arlen's house.

The Three Sailors' Gambit

Sitting some years ago in the ancient tavern at Over, one afternoon in Spring, I was waiting, as was my custom, for something strange to happen. In this I was not always disappointed for the very curious leaded panes of that tavern, facing the sea, let a light into the low-ceilinged room so mysterious, particularly at evening, that it somehow seemed to affect the events within. Be that as it may, I have seen strange things in that tavern and heard stranger things told.

And as I sat there three sailors entered the tavern, just back, as they said, from sea, and come with sunburned skins from a very long voyage to the South; and one of them had a board and chessmen under his arm, and they were complaining that they could find no one who knew how to play chess.

This was the year that the Tournament was in England. And a little dark man at a table in a corner of the room, drinking sugar and water, asked them why they wished to play chess; and they said they would play any man for a pound. They opened their box of chessmen then, a cheap and nasty set, and the man refused to play with such uncouth pieces, and the sailors suggested that perhaps he could find better ones; and in the end he went round to his lodgings near by and brought his own, and then they sat down to play for a pound a side. It was a consultation game on the part of the sailors, they said that all three must play.

Well, the little dark man turned out to be Stavlokratz. Of course he was fabulously poor, and the sovereign meant more to him than it did to the sailors, but he didn't seem keen to play, it was the sailors that insisted; he had made the badness of the sailors' chessmen an excuse for not playing at all, but the sailors had over-ruled that, and then he told them straight out who he was, and the sailors had never heard of Stavlokratz.

Well, no more was said after that. Stavlokratz said no more, either because he did not wish to boast or because he was huffed that they did not know who he was. And I saw no reason to enlighten the sailors about him; if he took their pound they had brought it upon themselves, and my boundless admiration for his genius made me feel that he deserved whatever might come his way. He had not asked to play, they had named the stakes, he had warned them, and gave them the first move; there was nothing unfair about Stavlokratz.

I had never seen Stavlokratz before, but I had played over nearly every one of his games in the World Championship for the last three or four years; he was always of course the model chosen by students. Only young chess-players can appreciate my delight at seeing him play first hand.

Well, the sailors used to lower their heads almost as low as the table and mutter together before every move, but they muttered so low that you could not hear what they planned. They lost three pawns almost straight off, then a knight, and shortly after a bishop; they were playing in fact the famous Three Sailors' Gambit.

Stavlokratz was playing with the easy confidence that they say was usual with him, when suddenly at about the thirteenth move I saw him look surprised; he leaned forward and looked at the board and then at the sailors, but he learned nothing from their vacant faces; he looked back at the board again.

He moved more deliberately after that; the sailors lost two more pawns, Stavlokratz had lost nothing as yet. He looked at me I thought almost irritably, as though something would happen that he wished I was not there to see. I believed at first that he had qualms about taking the sailors' pound, until it dawned on me that he might lose the game; I saw that possibility in his face, not on the board, for the game had become almost incomprehensible to me. I cannot describe my astonishment. And a few moves later Stavlokratz resigned.

The sailors showed no more elation than if they had won some game with greasy cards, playing amongst themselves.

Stavlokratz asked them where they got their opening. "We kind of thought of it," said one. "It just come into our heads like," said another. He asked them questions about the ports they had touched at. He evidently thought as I did myself that they had learned their extraordinary gambit, perhaps in some old dependancy of Spain, from some young master of chess whose fame had not reached Europe. He was very eager to find out who this man could be, for neither of us imagined that those sailors had invented it, nor would anyone who had seen them. But he got no information from the sailors.

Stavlokratz could very ill afford the loss of a pound. He offered to play them again for the same stakes. The sailors began to set up the white pieces. Stavlokratz pointed out that it was his turn for the first move. The sailors agreed but continued to set up the white pieces and sat with the white before them waiting for him to move. It was a trivial incident, but it revealed to Stavlokratz and myself that none of these sailors was aware that white always moves first.

Stavlokratz played them on his own opening, reasoning of course that as they had never heard of Stavlokratz they would not know of his opening; and with probably a very good hope of getting back his pound he played the fifth variation with its tricky seventh move, at least so he intended, but it turned to a variation unknown to the students of Stavlokratz.

Throughout this game I watched the sailors closely, and I became sure, as only an attentive watcher can be, that the one on their left, Jim Bunion, did not even know the moves.

When I had made up my mind about this I watched only the other two, Adam Bailey and Bill Sloggs, trying to make out which was the master mind; and for a long while I could not. And then I heard Adam Bailey mutter six words, the only words I heard throughout the game, of all their consultations, "No, him with the horse's head." And I decided that Adam Bailey did not know what a knight was, though of course he might have been explaining things to Bill Sloggs, but it did not sound like that; so that left Bill Sloggs. I watched Bill Sloggs after that with a certain wonder; he was no more intellectual than the others to look at, though rather more forceful perhaps. Poor old Stavlokratz was beaten again.

Well, in the end I paid for Stavlokratz, and tried to get a game with Bill Sloggs alone, but this he would not agree to, it must be all three or none: and then I went back with Stavlokratz to his lodgings. He very kindly gave me a game: of course it did not last long but I am prouder of having been beaten by Stavlokratz than of any game that I have ever won. And then we talked for an hour about the sailors, and neither of us could make head or tail of them. I told him what I had noticed about Jim Bunion and Adam Bailey, and he agreed with me that Bill Sloggs was the man, though as to how he had come by that gambit or that variation of Stavlokratz's own opening he had no theory.

I had the sailors' address which was that tavern as much as anywhere, and they were to be there all evening. As evening drew in I went back to the tavern, and found there still the three sailors. And I offered Bill Sloggs two pounds for a game with him alone and he refused, but in the end he played me for a drink. And then I found that he had not heard of the "en passant" rule, and believed that the fact of checking the king prevented him from castling, and did not know that a player can have two or more queens on the board at the same time if he queens his pawns, or that a pawn could ever become a knight; and he made as many of the stock mistakes as he had time for in a short game, which I won. I thought that I should have got at the secret then, but his mates who had sat scowling all the while in the corner came up and interfered. It was a breach of their compact apparently for one to play by himself, at any rate they seemed angry. So I left the tavern then and came back again next day, and the next day and the day after, and often saw the sailors, but none were in a communicative mood. I had got Stavlokratz to keep away, and they could get no one to play chess with at a pound a side, and I would not play with them unless they told me the secret.

And then one evening I found Jim Bunion drunk, yet not so drunk as he wished, for the two pounds were spent; and I gave him very nearly a tumbler of whiskey, or what passed for whiskey in that tavern at Over, and he told me the secret at once. I had given the others some whiskey to keep them quiet, and later on in the evening they must have gone out, but Jim Bunion stayed with me by a little table leaning across it and talking low, right into my face, his breath smelling all the while of what passed for whiskey.

The wind was blowing outside as it does on bad nights in November, coming up with moans from the South, towards which the tavern faced with all its leaded panes, so that none but I was able to hear his voice as Jim Bunion gave up his secret.

They had sailed for years, he told me, with Bill Snyth; and on their last voyage home Bill Snyth had died. And he was buried at sea. Just the other side of the line they buried him, and his pals divided his kit, and these three got his crystal that only they knew he had, which Bill got one night in Cuba. They played chess with the crystal.

And he was going on to tell me about that night in Cuba when Bill had bought the crystal from the stranger, how some folks might think they had seen thunderstorms, but let them go and listen to that one that thundered in Cuba when Bill was buying his crystal and they'd find that they didn't know what thunder was. But then I interrupted him, unfortunately perhaps, for it broke the thread of his tale and set him rambling a while, and cursing other people and talking of other lands, China, Port Said and Spain: but I brought him back to Cuba again in the end. I asked him how they could play chess with a crystal; and he said that you looked at the board and looked at the crystal, and there was the game in the crystal the same as it was on the board, with all the odd little pieces looking just the same though smaller, horses' heads and whatnots; and as soon as the other man moved the move came out in the crystal, and then your move appeared after it, and all you had to do was to make it on the board. If you didn't make the move that you saw in the crystal things got very bad in it, everything horribly mixed and moving about rapidly, and scowling and making the same move over and over again, and the crystal getting cloudier and cloudier; it was best to take one's eyes away from it then, or one dreamt about it afterwards, and the foul little pieces came and cursed you in your sleep and moved about all night with their crooked moves.

I thought then that, drunk though he was, he was not telling the truth, and I promised to show him to people who played chess all their lives so that he and his mates could get a pound whenever they liked, and I promised not to reveal his secret even to Stavlokratz, if only he would tell me all the truth; and this promise I have kept till long after the three sailors have lost their secret. I told him straight out that I did not believe in the crystal. Well, Jim Bunion leaned forward then, even further across the table, and swore he had seen the man from whom Bill had bought the crystal and that he was one to whom anything was possible. To begin with his hair was villainously dark, and his features were unmistakable even down there in the South, and he could play chess with his eyes shut, and even then he could beat anyone in Cuba. But there was more than this, there was the bargain he made with Bill that told one who he was. He sold that crystal for Bill Snyth's soul.

Jim Bunion leaning over the table with his breath in my face nodded his head several times and was silent.

I began to question him then. Did they play chess as far away as Cuba? He said they all did. Was it conceivable that any man would make such a bargain as Snyth made? Wasn't the trick well known? Wasn't it in hundreds of books? And if he couldn't read books mustn't he have heard from sailors that it is the Devil's commonest dodge to get souls from silly people?

Jim Bunion had leant back in his own chair quietly smiling at my questions but when I mentioned silly people he leaned forward again, and thrust his face close to mine and asked me several times if I called Bill

Snyth silly. It seemed that these three sailors thought a great deal of Bill Snyth and it made Jim Bunion angry to hear anything said against him. I hastened to say that the bargain seemed silly though not of course the man who made it; for the sailor was almost threatening, and no wonder for the whiskey in that dim tavern would madden a nun.

When I said that the bargain seemed silly he smiled again, and then he thundered his fist down on the table and said that no one had ever yet got the best of Bill Snyth and that that was the worst bargain for himself that the Devil ever made, and that from all he had read or heard of the Devil he had never been so badly had before as the night when he met Bill Snyth at the inn in the thunderstorm in Cuba, for Bill Snyth already had the damndest soul at sea; Bill was a good fellow, but his soul was damned right enough, so he got the crystal for nothing.

Yes, he was there and saw it all himself, Bill Snyth in the Spanish inn and the candles flaring, and the Devil walking in and out of the rain, and then the bargain between those two old hands, and the Devil going out into the lightning, and the thunderstorm raging on, and Bill Snyth sitting chuckling to himself between the bursts of the thunder.

But I had more questions to ask and interrupted this reminiscence. Why did they all three always play together? And a look of something like fear came over Jim Bunion's face; and at first he would not speak. And then he said to me that it was like this; they had not paid for that crystal, but got it as their share of Bill Snyth's kit. If they had paid for it or given something in exchange to Bill Snyth that would have been all right, but they couldn't do that now because Bill was dead, and they were not sure if the old bargain might not hold good. And Hell must be a large and lonely place, and to go there alone must be bad, and so the three agreed that they would all stick together, and use the crystal all three or not at all, unless one died, and then the two would use it and the one that was gone would wait for them. And the last of the three to go would take the crystal with him, or maybe the crystal would bring him. They didn't think, they said, they were the kind of men for Heaven, and he hoped they knew their place better than that, but they didn't fancy the notion of

Hell alone, if Hell it had to be. It was all right for Bill Snyth, he was afraid of nothing. He had known perhaps five men that were not afraid of death, but Bill Snyth was not afraid of Hell. He died with a smile on his face like a child in its sleep; it was drink killed poor Bill Snyth.

This was why I had beaten Bill Sloggs; Sloggs had the crystal on him while we played, but would not use it; these sailors seemed to fear loneliness as some people fear being hurt; he was the only one of the three who could play chess at all, he had learnt it in order to be able to answer questions and keep up their pretence, but he had learnt it badly, as I found. I never saw the crystal, they never showed it to anyone; but Jim Bunion told me that night that it was about the size that the thick end of a hen's egg would be if it were round. And then he fell asleep.

There were many more questions that I would have asked him but I could not wake him up. I even pulled the table away so that he fell to the floor, but he slept on, and all the tavern was dark but for one candle burning; and it was then that I noticed for the first time that the other two sailors had gone, no one remained at all but Jim Bunion and I and the sinister barman of that curious inn, and he too was asleep.

When I saw that it was impossible to wake the sailor I went out into the night. Next day Jim Bunion would talk of it no more; and when I went back to Stavlokratz I found him already putting on paper his theory about the sailors, which became accepted by chess-players, that one of them had been taught their curious gambit and that the other two between them had learnt all the defensive openings as well as general play. Though who taught them no one could say, in spite of enquiries made afterwards all along the Southern Pacific.

I never learnt any more details from any of the three sailors, they were always too drunk to speak or else not drunk enough to be communicative. I seem just to have taken Jim Bunion at the flood. But I kept my promise, it was I that introduced them to the Tournament, and a pretty mess they made of established reputations. And so they kept on for months, never losing a game and always playing for their pound a side. I used to follow them wherever they went merely to watch their play. They were more marvellous than Stavlokratz even in his youth.

But then they took to liberties such as giving their queen when playing first-class players. And in the end one day when all three were drunk they played the best player in England with only a row of pawns. They won the game all right. But the ball broke to pieces. I never smelt such a stench in all my life.

The three sailors took it stoically enough, they signed on to different ships and went back again to the sea, and the world of chess lost sight, for ever I trust, of the most remarkable players it ever knew, who would have altogether spoiled the game.

The Exiles Club

It was an evening party; and something someone had said to me had started me talking about a subject that to me is full of fascination, the subject of old religions, forsaken gods. The truth (for all religions have some of it), the wisdom, the beauty, of the religions of countries to which I travel have not the same appeal to me; for one only notices in them their tyranny and intolerance and the abject servitude that they claim from thought; but when a dynasty has been dethroned in heaven and goes forgotten and outcast even among men, one's eyes no longer dazzled by its power find something very wistful in the faces of fallen gods suppliant to be remembered, something almost tearfully beautiful, like a long warm summer twilight fading gently away after some day memorable in the story of earthly wars. Between what Zeus, for instance, has been once and the half-remembered tale he is to-day there lies a space so great that there is no change of fortune known to man whereby we may measure the height down which he has fallen. And it is the same with many another god at whom once the ages trembled and the twentieth century treats as an old wives' tale. The fortitude that such a fall demands is surely more than human.

Some such things as these I was saying, and being upon a subject that much attracts me I possibly spoke too loudly, certainly I was not aware that standing close behind me was no less a person than the ex-King of Eritivaria, the thirty islands of the East, or I would have moderated my voice and moved away a little to give him more room. I was not aware of his presence until his satellite, one who had fallen with him into exile but still revolved about him, told me that his master desired to know me; and so to my surprise I was presented though neither of them even knew my name. And that was how I came to be invited by the ex-King to dine at his club.

At the time I could only account for his wishing to know me by supposing that he found in his own exiled condition some likeness to the fallen fortunes of the gods of whom I talked unwitting of his presence; but now I know that it was not of himself he was thinking when he asked me to dine at that club.

The club would have been the most imposing building in any street in London, but in that obscure mean quarter of London in which they had built it it appeared unduly enormous. Lifting right up above those grotesque houses and built in that Greek style that we call Georgian, there was something Olympian about it. To my host an unfashionable street could have meant nothing, through all his youth wherever he had gone had become fashionable the moment he went there; words like the East End could have had no meaning to him.

Whoever built that house had enormous wealth and cared nothing for fashion, perhaps despised it. As I stood gazing at the magnificent upper windows draped with great curtains, indistinct in the evening, on which huge shadows flickered my host attracted my attention from the doorway, and so I went in and met for the second time the ex-King of Eritivaria.

In front of us a stairway of rare marble led upwards, he took me through a side-door and downstairs and we came to a banqueting-hall of great magnificence. A long table ran up the middle of it, laid for quite twenty people, and I noticed the peculiarity that instead of chairs there were thrones for everyone except me, who was the only guest and for whom there was an ordinary chair. My host explained to me when we all sat down that everyone who belonged to that club was by rights a king.

In fact none was permitted, he told me, to belong to the club unless his claim to a kingdom made out in writing had been examined and allowed by those whose duty it was. The whim of a populace or the candidate's own misrule were never considered by the investigators, nothing counted with them but heredity and lawful descent from kings, all else was ignored. At that table there were those who had once reigned themselves, others lawfully claimed descent from kings that the world had forgotten, the kingdoms claimed by some had even changed their names. Hatzgurh, the mountain kingdom, is almost regarded as mythical.

I have seldom seen greater splendour than that long hall provided below the level of the street. No doubt by day it was a little sombre, as all basements are, but at night with its great crystal chandeliers, and the glitter of heirlooms that had gone into exile, it surpassed the splendour of palaces that have only one king. They had come to London suddenly most of those kings, or their fathers before them, or forefathers; some had come away from their kingdoms by night, in a light sleigh, flogging the horses, or had galloped clear with morning over the border, some had trudged roads for days from their capital in disguise, yet many had had time just as they left to snatch up some small thing without price in markets, for the sake of old times as they said, but quite as much, I thought, with an eye to the future. And there these treasures glittered on that long table in the banqueting-hall of the basement of that strange club. Merely to see them was much, but to hear their story that their owners told was to go back in fancy to epic times on the romantic border of fable and fact, where the heroes of history fought with the gods of myth. The famous silver horses of Gilgianza were there climbing their sheer mountain, which they did by miraculous means before the time of the Goths. It was not a large piece of silver but its workmanship outrivaled the skill of the bees.

A yellow Emperor had brought out of the East a piece of that incomparable porcelain that had made his dynasty famous though all their deeds are forgotten, it had the exact shade of the right purple.

And there was a little golden statuette of a dragon stealing a diamond from a lady, the dragon had the diamond in his claws, large and of the first water. There had been a kingdom whose whole constitution and history were founded on the legend, from which alone its kings had claimed their right to the sceptre, that a dragon stole a diamond from a lady. When its last king left that country, because his favourite general used a peculiar formation under the fire of artillery, he brought with him the little ancient image that no longer proved him a king outside that singular club.

There was the pair of amethyst cups of the turbaned King of Foo, the one that he drank from himself, and the one that he gave to his enemies, eye could not tell which was which.

All these things the ex-King of Eritivaria showed me, telling me a marvellous tale of each; of his own he had brought nothing, except the mascot that used once to sit on the top of the water tube of his favourite motor.

I have not outlined a tenth of the splendour of that table, I had meant to come again and examine each piece of plate and make notes of its history; had I known that this was the last time I should wish to enter that club I should have looked at its treasures more attentively, but now as the wine went round and the exiles began to talk I took my eyes from the table and listened to strange tales of their former state.

He that has seen better times was usually a poor tale to tell, some mean and trivial thing that has been his undoing, but they that dined in that basement had mostly fallen like oaks on nights of abnormal tempest, had fallen mightily and shaken a nation. Those who had not been kings themselves, but claimed through an exiled ancestor, had stories to tell of even grander disaster, history seeming to have mellowed their dynasty's fate as moss grows over an oak a great while fallen. There were no jealousies there as so often there are among kings, rivalry must have ceased with the loss of their navies and armies, and they showed no bitterness against those that had turned them out, one speaking of the error of his Prime Minister by which he had lost his throne as "poor old Friedrich's Heaven-sent gift of tactlessness."

They gossiped pleasantly of many things, the tittle-tattle we all had to know when we were learning history, and many a wonderful story I might have heard, many a side-light on mysterious wars had I not made use of one unfortunate word. That word was "upstairs."

The ex-King of Eritivaria having pointed out to me those unparalleled heirlooms to which I have alluded, and many more besides, hospitably asked me if there was anything else that I would care to see, he meant the pieces of plate that they had in the cupboards, the curiously graven swords of other princes, historic jewels, legendary seals, but I who had had a glimpse of their marvelous staircase, whose balustrade I believed to be solid gold and wondering why in such a stately house they chose to dine in the basement, mentioned the word "upstairs." A profound hush came down on the whole assembly, the hush that might greet levity in a cathedral.

"Upstairs!" he gasped, "We cannot go upstairs."

I perceived that what I had said was an ill-chosen thing. I tried to excuse myself but knew not how. "Of course," I muttered, "members may not take guests upstairs."

"Members!" he said to me, "We are not the members!" There was such reproof in his voice that I said no more, I looked at him questioningly, perhaps my lips moved, I may have said, "What are you?" A great surprise had come on me at their attitude.

"We are the waiters," he said.

That I could not have known, here at least was honest ignorance that I had no need to be ashamed of, the very opulence of their table denied it.

"Then who are the members?" I asked.

Such a hush fell at that question, such a hush of genuine awe, that all of a sudden a wild thought entered my head, a thought strange and fantastic and terrible. I gripped my host by the wrist and hushed my voice.

"Are they too exiles?" I asked.

Twice as he looked in my face he gravely nodded his head. I left that club very swiftly indeed, never to see it again, scarcely pausing to say farewell to those menial kings, and as I left the door a great window opened far up at the top of the house and a flash of lightning streamed from it and killed a dog.

Where the Tides Ebb and Flow

I dreamt that I had done a horrible thing, so that burial was to be denied me either in soil or sea, neither could there be any hell for me.

I waited for some hours, knowing this. Then my friends came for me, and slew me secretly and with ancient rite, and lit great tapers, and carried me away.

It was all in London that the thing was done, and they went furtively at dead of night along grey streets and among mean houses until they came to the river. And the river and the tide of the sea were grappling with one another between the mud-banks, and both of them were black and full of lights. A sudden wonder came into the eyes of each, as my friends came near to them with their glaring tapers. All these things I saw as they carried me dead and stiffening, for my soul was still among my bones, because there was no hell for it, and because Christian burial was denied me.

They took me down a stairway that was green with slimy things, and so came slowly to the terrible mud. There, in the territory of forsaken things, they dug a shallow grave. When they had finished they laid me in the grave, and suddenly they cast their tapers to the river. And when the water had quenched the flaring lights the tapers looked pale and small as they bobbed upon the tide, and at once the glamour of the calamity was gone, and I noticed then the approach of the huge dawn; and my friends cast their cloaks over their faces, and the solemn procession was turned into many fugitives that furtively stole away.

Then the mud came back wearily and covered all but my face. There I lay alone with quite forgotten things, with drifting things that the tides will take no farther, with useless things and lost things, and the horrible unnatural bricks that are neither stone nor soil. I was rid of feeling, because I had been killed, but perception and thought were in my unhappy soul. The dawn widened, and I saw the desolate houses that crowded the marge of the river, and their dead windows peered into my dead eyes, windows with bales behind them instead of human souls. I grew so weary looking at these forlorn things that I wanted to cry out, but could not, because I was dead. Then I knew, as I had never known before, that for all the years that herd of desolate houses had wanted to cry out too, but, being dead, were dumb. And I knew then that it had yet been well with the forgotten drifting things if they had wept, but they were eyeless and without life. And I, too, tried to weep, but there were no tears in my dead eyes. And I knew then that the river might have cared for us, might have caressed us, might have sung to us, but he swept broadly onwards, thinking of nothing but the princely ships.

At last the tide did what the river would not, and came and covered me over, and my soul had rest in the green water, and rejoiced and believed that it had the Burial of the Sea. But with the ebb the water fell again, and left me alone again with the callous mud among the forgotten things that drift no more, and with the sight of all those desolate houses, and with the knowledge among all of us that each was dead.

In the mournful wall behind me, hung with green weeds, forsaken of the sea, dark tunnels appeared, and secret narrow passages that were clamped and barred. From these at last the stealthy rats came down to nibble me away, and my soul rejoiced thereat and believed that he would be free perforce from the accursed bones to which burial was refused.

Very soon the rats ran away a little space and whispered among themselves. They never came any more. When I found that I was accursed even among the rats I tried to weep again.

Then the tide came swinging back and covered the dreadful mud, and hid the desolate houses, and soothed the forgotten things, and my soul had ease for a while in the sepulture of the sea. And then the tide forsook me again.

To and fro it came about me for many years. Then the County Council found me, and gave me decent burial. It was the first grave that I had ever slept in. That very night my friends came for me. They dug me up and put me back again in the shallow hole in the mud.

Again and again through the years my bones found burial, but always behind the funeral lurked one of those terrible men who, as soon as night fell, came and dug them up and carried them back again to the hole in the mud.

And then one day the last of those men died who once had done to me this terrible thing. I heard his soul go over the river at sunset.

And again I hoped.

A few weeks afterwards I was found once more, and once more taken out of that restless place and given deep burial in sacred ground, where my soul hoped that it should rest.

Almost at once men came with cloaks and tapers to give me back to the mud, for the thing had become a tradition and a rite. And all the forsaken things mocked me in their dumb hearts when they saw me carried back, for they were jealous of me because I had left the mud. It must be remembered that I could not weep.

And the years went by seawards where the black barges go, and the great derelict centuries became lost at sea, and still I lay there without any cause to hope, and daring not to hope without a cause, because of the terrible envy and the anger of the things that could drift no more.

Once a great storm rode up, even as far as London, out of the sea from the South; and he came curving into the river with the fierce East wind. And he was mightier than the dreary tides, and went with great leaps over the listless mud. And all the sad forgotten things rejoiced, and mingled with things that were haughtier than they, and rode once more amongst the lordly shipping that was driven up and down. And out of their hideous home he took my bones, never again, I hoped, to be vexed with the ebb and flow. And with the fall of the tide he went riding down the river and turned to the southwards, and so went to his home. And my bones he scattered among many isles and along the shores of happy alien mainlands. And for a moment, while they were far asunder, my soul was almost free.

Then there arose, at the will of the moon, the assiduous flow of the tide, and it undid at once the work of the ebb, and gathered my bones from the marge of sunny isles, and gleaned them all along the mainland's shores, and went rocking northwards till it came to the mouth of the Thames, and there turned westwards its relentless face, and so went up the river and came to the hole in the mud, and into it dropped my bones; and partly the mud covered them and partly it left them white, for the mud cares not for its forsaken things.

Then the ebb came, and I saw the dead eyes of the houses and the jealousy of the other forgotten things that the storm had not carried thence.

And some more centuries passed over the ebb and flow and over the loneliness of things forgotten. And I lay there all the whole in the careless grip of the mud, never wholly covered, yet never able to go free, and I longed for the great caress of the warm Earth or the comfortable lap of the Sea.

Sometimes men found my bones and buried them, but the tradition never died, and my friends' successors always brought them back. At last the barges went no more, and there were fewer lights; shaped timbers no longer floated down the fair-way, and there came instead old wind-uprooted trees in all their natural simplicity.

At last I was aware that somewhere near me a blade of grass was growing, and the moss began to appear all over the dead houses. One day some thistledown went drifting over the river.

For some years I watched these signs attentively, until I became certain that London was passing away. Then I hoped once more, and all along both banks of the river there was anger among the lost things that anything should dare to hope upon the forsaken mud. Gradually the horrible houses crumbled, until the poor dead things that never had had life got decent burial among the weeds and moss. At last the may appeared and the convolvulus. Finally, the wild rose stood up over mounds that had been wharves and warehouses. Then I knew that the cause of Nature had triumphed, and London had passed away.

The last man in London came to the wall by the river, in an ancient cloak that was one of those that once my friends had worn, and peered over the edge to see that I still was there. Then he went, and I never saw men again: they had passed away with London.

A few days after the last man had gone the birds came into London, all the birds that sing. When they first saw me they all looked sideways at me, then they went away a little and spoke among themselves.

"He only sinned against Man," they said; "it is not our quarrel."

"Let us be kind to him," they said.

Then they hopped nearer me and began to sing. It was the time of the rising of the dawn, and from both banks of the river, and from the sky, and from the thickets that were once the streets, hundreds of birds were singing. As the light increased the birds sang more and more; they grew thicker and thicker in the air above my head, till there were thousands of them singing there, and then millions, and at last I could see nothing but a host of flickering wings with the sunlight on them, and little gaps of sky. Then when there was nothing to be heard in London but the myriad notes of that exultant song, my soul rose up from the bones in the hole in the mud and began to climb up the song heavenwards. And it seemed that a laneway opened amongst the wings of the birds, and it went up and up, and one of the smaller gates of Paradise stood ajar at the end of it. And then I knew by a sign that the mud should receive me no more, for suddenly I found that I could weep.

At this moment I opened my eyes in bed in a house in London, and outside some sparrows were twittering in a tree in the light of the radiant morning; and there were tears still wet upon my face, for one's restraint is feeble while one sleeps. But I arose and opened the window wide, and, stretching my hands out over the little garden, I blessed the birds whose song had woken me up from the troubled and terrible centuries of my dream.

The Field

When one has seen Spring's blossom fall in London, and Summer appear and ripen and decay, as it does early in cities, and one is in London still, then, at some moment or other, the country places lift their flowery heads and call to one with an urgent, masterful clearness, upland behind upland in the twilight like to some heavenly choir arising rank on rank to call a drunkard from his gambling-bell. No volume of traffic can drown the sound of it, no lure of London can weaken its appeal. Having heard it one's fancy is gone, and evermore departed, to some coloured pebble a-gleam in a rural brook, and all that London can offer is swept from one's mind like some suddenly smitten metropolitan Goliath.

The call is from afar both in leagues and years, for the hills that call one are the hills that were, and their voices are the voices of long ago, when the elf-kings still had horns. I see them now, those hills of my infancy (for it is they that call), with their faces upturned to the purple twilight, and the faint diaphanous figures of the fairies peering out from under the bracken to see if evening is come. I do not see upon their regal summits those desirable mansions, and highly desirable residences, which have lately been built for gentlemen who would exchange customers for tenants.

When the hills called I used to go to them by road, riding a bicycle. If you go by train you miss the gradual approach, you do not cast off London like an old forgiven sin, nor pass by little villages on the way that must have some rumour of the hills; nor, wondering if they are still the same, come at last upon the edge of their far-spread robes, and so on to their feet, and see far off their holy, welcoming faces. In the train you see them suddenly round a curve, and there they all are sitting in the sun.

I imagine that as one penetrated out from some enormous forest of the tropics, the wild beasts would become fewer, the gloom would lighten, and the horror of the place would slowly lift. Yet as one emerges nearer to the edge of London, and nearer to the beautiful influence of the hills, the houses become uglier, the streets viler, the gloom deepens, the errors of civilisation stand bare to the scorn of the fields.

Where ugliness reaches the height of its luxuriance, in the dense misery of the place, where one imagines the builder saying, "Here I culminate. Let us give thanks to Satan," there is a bridge of yellow brick, and through it, as through some gate of filigree silver opening on fairyland, one passes into the country.

To left and right, as far as one can see, stretches that monstrous city; before one are the fields like an old, old song.

There is a field there that is full of king-cups. A stream runs through it, and along the stream is a little wood of oziers. There I used often to rest at the stream's edge before my long journey to the hills.

There I used to forget London, street by street. Sometimes I picked a bunch of king-cups to show them to the hills.

I often came there. At first I noticed nothing about the field except its beauty and its peacefulness.

But the second time that I came I thought there was something ominous about the field.

Down there among the king-cups by the little shallow stream I felt that something terrible might happen in just such a place.

I did not stay long there, because I thought that too much time spent in London had brought on these morbid fancies and I went on to the hills as fast as I could.

I stayed for some days in the country air, and when I came back I went to the field again to enjoy that peaceful spot before entering London. But there was still something ominous among the oziers.

A year elapsed before I went there again. I emerged from the shadow of London into the gleaming sun, the bright green grass and the king-cups were flaming in the light, and the little stream was singing a happy song. But the moment I stepped into the field my old uneasiness returned, and worse than before. It was as though the shadow was brooding there of some dreadful future thing, and a year had brought it nearer. I reasoned that the exertion of bïcycling might be bad for one, and that the moment one rested this uneasiness might result.

A little later I came back past the field by night, and the song of the stream in the hush attracted me down to it. And there the fancy came to me that it would be a terribly cold place to be in in the starlight, if for some reason one was hurt and could not get away. I knew a man who was minutely acquainted with the past history of that locality, and him I asked if anything historical had ever happened in that field. When he pressed me for my reason in asking him this, I said that the field had seemed to me such a good place to hold a pageant in. But he said that nothing of any interest had ever occurred there, nothing at all.

So it was from the future that the field's trouble came. For three years off and on I made visits to the field, and every time more clearly it boded evil things, and my uneasiness grew more acute every time that I was lured to go and rest among the cool green grass under the beautiful oziers. Once to distract my thoughts I tried to gauge how fast the stream was trickling, but I found myself wondering if it flowed faster than blood.

I felt that it would be a terrible place to go mad in, one would hear voices.

At last I went to a poet whom I knew, and woke him from huge dreams, and put before him the whole case of the field. He had not been out of London all that year, and he promised to come with me and look at the field, and tell me what was going to happen there. It was late in July when we went. The pavement, the air, the houses and the dirt had been all baked dry by the summer, the weary traffic dragged on, and on, and on, and Sleep spreading her wings soared up and floated from London and went to walk beautifully in rural places.

When the poet saw the field he was delighted, the flowers were out in masses all along the stream, he went down to the little wood rejoicing. By the side of the stream he stood and seemed very sad. Once or twice he looked up and down it mournfully, then he bent and looked at the king-cups, first one and then another, very closely, and shaking his head.

For a long while he stood in silence, and all my old uneasiness returned, and my bodings for the future.

And then I said "What manner of field is it?"

And he shook his head sorrowfully.

"It is a battlefield," he said.

A Tale of London

"Come," said the Sultan to his hasheesh-eater in the very furthest lands that know Bagdad, "dream to me now of London."

And the hasheesh-eater made a low obeisance and seated himself cross-legged upon a purple cushion broidered with golden poppies, on the floor, beside an ivory bowl where the hasheesh was, and having eaten liberally of the hasheesh blinked seven times and spoke thus:

"O Friend of God, know then that London is the desiderate town even of all Earth's cities. Its houses are of ebony and cedar which they roof with thin copper plates that the hand of Time turns green. They have golden balconies in which amethysts are where they sit and watch the sunset. Musicians in the gloaming steal softly along the ways; unheard their feet fall on the white sea-sand with which those ways are strewn, and in the darkness suddenly they play on dulcimers and instruments with strings. Then are there murmurs in the balconies praising their skill, then are there bracelets cast down to them for reward and golden necklaces and even pearls.

"Indeed but the city is fair; there is by the sandy ways a paving all alabaster, and the lanterns along it are of chrysoprase, all night long they shine green, but of amethyst are the lanterns of the balconies.

"As the musicians go along the ways dancers gather aboutthem and dance upon the alabaster pavings, for joy and not for hire. Sometimes a window opens far up in an ebony palace and a wreath is cast down to a dancer or orchids showered upon them.

"Indeed of many cities have I dreamt but of none fairer, through many marble metropolitan gates hasheesh has led me, but London is its secret, the last gate of all; the ivory bowl has nothing more to show. And indeed even now the imps that crawl behind me and that will not let me be are plucking me by the elbow and bidding my spirit return, for well they know that I have seen too much. `No, not London,' they say; and therefore I will speak of some other city, a city of some less mysterious land, and anger not the imps with forbidden things. I will speak of Persepolis or famous Thebes."

A shade of annoyance crossed the Sultan's face, a look of thunder that you had scarcely seen, but in those lands they watched his visage well, and though his spirit was wandering far away and his eyes were bleared with hasheesh yet that storyteller there and then perceived the look that was death, and sent his spirit back at once to London as a man runs into his house when the thunder comes.

"And therefore," he continued, "in the desiderate city, in London, all their camels are pure white. Remarkable is the swiftness of their horses, that draw their chariots that are of ivory along those sandy ways and that are of surpassing lightness, they have little bells of silver upon their horses' heads. O Friend of God, if you perceived their merchants! The glory of their dresses in the noonday! They are no less gorgeous than those butterflies that float about their streets. They have overcloaks of green and vestments of azure, huge purple flowers blaze on their overcloaks, the work of cunning needles, the centres of the flowers are of gold and the petals of purple. All their hats are black —" ("No, no," said the Sultan) - "but irises are set about the brims, and green plumes float above the crowns of them.

"They have a river that is named the Thames, on it their ships go up with violet sails bringing incense for the braziers that perfume the streets, new songs exchanged for gold with alien tribes, raw silver for the statues of their heroes, gold to make balconies where the women sit, great sapphires to reward their poets with, the secrets of old cities and strange lands, the learning of the dwellers in far isles, emeralds, diamonds, and the hoards of the sea. And whenever a ship comes into port and furls its violet sails and the news spreads through London that she has come, then all the merchants go down to the river to barter, and all day long the chariots whirl through the streets, and the sound of their going is a mighty roar all day until evening, their roar is even like—"

"Not so," said the Sultan.

"Truth is not hidden from the Friend of God," replied the hasheesh-eater, "I have erred being drunken with the hasheesh, for in the desiderate city, even in London, so thick upon the ways is the white sea-sand with which the city glimmers that no sound comes from the path of the charioteers, but they go softly like a light sea-wind." ("It is well," said the Sultan.) "They go softly down to the port where the vessels are, and the merchandise in from the sea, amongst the wonders that the sailors show, on land by the high ships, and softly they go though swiftly at evening back to their homes.

"O would that the Munificent, the Illustrious, the Friend of God, had even seen these things, had seen the jewellers with their empty baskets, bargaining there by the ships, when the barrels of emeralds came up from the hold. Or would that he had seen the fountains there in silver basins in the midst of the ways. I have seen small spires upon their ebony houses and the spires were all of gold, birds strutted there upon the copper roofs from golden spire to spire that have no equal for splendour in all the woods of the world. And over London the desiderate city the sky is so deep a blue that by this alone the traveller may know where he has come, and may end his fortunate journey. Nor yet for any colour of the sky is there too great heat in London, for along its ways a wind blows always from the South gently and cools the city.

"Such, O Friend of God, is indeed the city of London, lying very far off on the yonder side of Bagdad, without a peer for beauty or excellence of its ways among the towns of the earth or cities of song; and even so, as I have told, its fortunate citizens dwell, with their hearts ever devising beautiful things and from the beauty of their own fair work that is more abundant around them every year, receiving new inspirations to work things more beautiful yet."

"And is their government good?" the Sultan said.

"It is most good," said the hasheesh-eater, and fell backwards upon the floor.

He lay thus and was silent. And when the Sultan perceived he would speak no more that night he smiled and lightly applauded.

And there was envy in that palace, in lands beyond Bagdad, of all that dwell in London.

A Narrow Escape

It was underground.

In that dank cavern down below Belgrave Square the walls were dripping. But what was that to the magician? It was secrecy that he needed, not dryness. There he pondered upon the trend of events, shaped destinies and concocted magical brews.

For the last few years the serenity of his ponderings had been disturbed by the noise of the motor-bus; while to his keen ears there came the sound of the earthquake-rumble, far off, of the train in the tube, going down Sloane Street; and when he heard of the world above his head was not to its credit.

He decided one evening over his evil pipe, down there in his dank chamber, that London had lived long enough, had abused its opportunities, had gone too far, in fine, with its civilisation. And so he decided to wreck it.

Therefore he beckoned up his acolyte from the weedy end of the cavern, and "Bring me," he said, "the heart of the toad that dwelleth in Arabia and by the mountains of Bethany." The acolyte slipped away by the hidden door, leaving that grim old man with his frightful pipe, and whither he went who knows but the gipsy people, or by what path he returned; but within a year he stood in the cavern again, slipping secretly in by the trap while the old man smoked, and he brought with him a little fleshy thing that rotted in a casket of pure gold.

"What is it?" the old man croaked.

"It is," said the acolyte, "the heart of the toad that dwelt once in Arabia and by the mountains of Bethany."

The old man's crooked fingers closed on it, and he blessed the acolyte with his rasping voice and claw-like hand uplifted; the motor-bus rumbled above on its endless journey; far off the train shook Sloane Street.

"Come," said the old magician, "it is time." And there and then they left the weedy cavern, the acolyte carrying cauldron, gold poker and all things needful, and went abroad in the light. And very wonderful the old man looked in his silks.

Their goal was the outskirts of London; the old man strode in front and the acolyte ran behind him, and there was something magical in the old man's stride alone, without his wonderful dress, the cauldron and wand, the hurrying acolyte and the small gold poker.

Little boys jeered till they caught the old man's eye. So there went through London this strange procession of two, too swift for any to follow. Things seemed worse up there than they did in the cavern, and the further they got on their way towards London's outskirts the worse London got. "It is time," said the old man, "surely."

And so they came at last to London's edge and a small hill watching it with a mournful look. It was so mean that the acolyte longed for the cavern, dank though it was and full of terrible sayings that the old man said when he slept.

They climbed the hill and put the cauldron down, and put there in the necessary things, and lit a fire of herbs that no chemist will sell nor decent gardener grow, and stirred the cauldron with the golden poker. The magician retired a little apart and muttered, then he strode back to the cauldron and, all being ready, suddenly opened the casket and let the fleshy thing fall in to boil.

Then he made spells, then he flung up his arms; the fumes from the cauldron entering in at his mind he said raging things that he had not known before and runes that were dreadful (the acolyte screamed); there he cursed London from fog to loam-pit, from zenith to the abyss, motor-bus, factory, shop, parliament, people. "Let them all perish," he said, "and London pass away, tram lines and bricks and pavement, the usurpers too long of the fields, let them all pass away and the wild hares come back, blackberry and briar-rose."

"Let it pass," he said, "pass now, pass utterly."

In the momentary silence the old man coughed, then waited with eager eyes; and the long hum of London hummed as it always has since first the reed-huts were set up by the river, changing its note at times but always humming, louder now than it was in years gone by, but humming night and day though its voice be cracked with age; so it hummed on.

And the old man turned him round to his trembling acolyte and terribly said as he sank into the earth: "YOU HAVE NOT BROUGHT ME THE HEART OF THE TOAD THAT DWELLETH IN ARABIA NOR BY THE MOUNTAINS OF BETHANY!"

Bethmoora

There is a faint freshness in the London night as though some strayed reveller of a breeze had left his comrades in the Kentish uplands and had entered the town by stealth. The pavements are a little damp and shiny. Upon one's ears that at this late hour have become very acute there hits the tap of a remote footfall. Louder and louder grow the taps, filling the whole night. And a black cloaked figure passes by, and goes tapping into the dark. One who has danced goes homewards. Somewhere a ball has closed its doors and ended. Its yellow lights are out, its musicians are silent, its dancers have all gone into the night air, and Time has said of it, "Let it be past and over, and among the things that I have put away."

Shadows begin to detach themselves from their great gathering places. No less silently than those shadows that are thin and dead move homewards the stealthy cats. Thus have we even in London our faint forebodings of the dawn's approach, which the birds and the beasts and the stars are crying aloud to the untrammelled fields.

At what moment I know not I perceive that the night itself is irrecoverably overthrown. It is suddenly revealed to me by the weary pallor of the street lamps that the streets are silent and nocturnal still, not because there is any strength in night, but because men have not yet arisen from sleep to defy him. So have I seen dejected and untidy guards still bearing antique muskets in palatial gateways, although the realms of the monarch that they guard have shrunk to a single province which no enemy yet has troubled to overrun.

And it is now manifest from the aspect of the street lamps, those abashed dependants of night, that already English mountain peaks have seen the dawn, that the cliffs of Dover are standing white to the morning, that the sea-mist has lifted and is pouring inland. And now men with a hose have come and are sluicing out the streets.

Behold now night is dead.

What memories, what fancies throng one's mind! A night but just now gathered out of London by the hostile hand of Time. A million common artificial things all cloaked for a while in mystery, like beggars robed in purple, and seated on dread thrones. Four million people asleep, dreaming perhaps. What worlds have they gone into? Whom have they met? But my thoughts are far off with Bethmoora in her loneliness, whose gates swing to and fro. To and fro they swing, and creak and creak in the wind, but no one hears them. They are of green copper, very lovely, but no one sees them now. The desert wind pours sand into their hinges, no watchman comes to ease them. No guard goes round Bethmoora's battlements, no enemy assails them. There are no lights in her houses, no footfall in her streets; she stands there dead and lonely beyond the Hills of Hap, and I would see Bethmoora once again, but dare not.

It is many a year, as they tell me, since Bethmoora became desolate. Her desolation is spoken of in taverns where sailors meet, and certain travellers have told me of it.

I had hoped to see Bethmoora once again. It is many a year ago, they say, when the vintage was last gathered in from the vineyards that I knew, where it is all desert now. It was a radiant day, and the people of the city were dancing by the vineyards, while here and there one played upon the kalipac. The purple flowering shrubs were all in bloom, and the snow shone upon the Hills of Hap.

Outside the copper gates they crushed the grapes in vats to make the syrabub. It had been a goodly vintage.

In little gardens at the desert's edge men beat the tambang and the tittibuk, and blew melodiously the zootibar.

All there was mirth and song and dance, because the vintage had been gathered in, and there would be ample syrabub for the winter months, and much left over to exchange for turquoises and emeralds with the merchants who come down from Oxuhahn. Thus they rejoiced all day over their vintage on the narrow strip of cultivated ground that lay between Bethmoora and the desert which meets the sky to the South. And when the heat of the day began to abate, and the sun drew near to the snows on the Hills of Hap, the note of the zootibar still rose clear from the gardens, and the brilliant dresses of the dancers still wound among the flowers. All that day three men on mules had been noticed crossing the face of the Hills of Hap. Backwards and forwards they moved as the track wound lower and lower, three little specks of black against the snow. They were seen first in the very early morning up near the shoulder of Peol Jagganoth, and seemed to be coming out of Utnar Vehi. All day they came. And in the evening, just before lights come out and colours change, they appeared before Bethmoora's copper gates. They carried staves, such as messengers bear in those lands, and seemed sombrely clad when the dancers all came round them with their green and lilac dresses. Those Europeans who were present and heard the message given were ignorant of the language, and only caught the name of Utnar Vehi. But it was brief, and passed rapidly from mouth to mouth, and almost at once the people burnt their vineyards and began to flee away from Bethmoora, going for the most part northwards, though some went to the East. They ran down out of their fair white houses, and streamed through the copper gate; the throbbing of the tambang and the tittibuk suddenly ceased with the note of the zootibar, and the clinking kalipac stopped a moment after. The three strange travellers went back the way they came the instant their message was given. It was the hour when a light would have appeared in some high tower, and window after window would have poured into the dusk its lion-frightening light, and the copper gates would have been fastened up. But no lights came out in windows there that night and have not ever since, and those copper gates were left wide and have never shut, and the sound arose of the red fire crackling in the vineyards, and the pattering of feet fleeing softly. There were no cries, no other sounds at all, only the rapid and determined flight. They fled as swiftly and quietly as a herd of wild cattle flee when they suddenly see a man. It was as though something had befallen which had been feared for generations, which could only be escaped by instant flight, which left no time for indecision.

Then fear took the Europeans also, and they too fled.

And what the message was I have never heard.

Many believe that it was a message from Thuba Mleen, the mysterious emperor of those lands, who is never seen by man, advising that Bethmoora should be left desolate. Others say that the message was one of warning from the gods, whether from friendly gods or from adverse ones they know not.

And others hold that the Plague was ravaging a line of cities over in Utnar Vehi, following the South-west wind which for many weeks had been blowing across them towards Bethmoora.

Some say that the terrible gnousar sickness was upon the three travellers, and that their very mules were dripping with it, and suppose that they were driven to the city by hunger, but suggest no better reason for so terrible a crime.

But most believe that it was a message from the desert himself, who owns all the Earth to the southwards, spoken with his peculiar cry to those three who knew his voice -men who had been out on the sand-wastes without tents by night, who had been by day without water, men who had been out there where the desert mutters, and had grown to know his needs and his malevolence. They say that the desert had a need for Bethmoora, that he wished to come into her lovely streets, and to send into her temples and her houses his storm-winds draped with sand. For he hates the sound and the sight of men in his old evil heart, and he would have Bethmoora silent and undisturbed, save for the weird love he whispers at her gates.

If I knew what that message was that the three men brought on mules, and told in the copper gate, I think that I should go and see Bethmoora once again. For a great longing comes on me here in London to see once more that white and beautiful city; and yet I dare not, for I know not the danger I should have to face, whether I should risk the fury of unknown dreadful gods, or some disease unspeakable and slow, or the desert's curse, or torture in some little private room of the Emperor Thuba Mleen, or something that the travellers have not told — perhaps more fearful still.

The Hashish Man

I was at a dinner in London the other day. The ladies had gone upstairs, and no one sat on my right; on my left there was a man I did not know, but he knew my name somehow apparently, for he turned to me after a while, and said, "I read a story of yours about Bethmoora in a review."

Of course I remembered the tale. It was about a beautiful Oriental city that was suddenly deserted in a day — nobody quite knew why. I said, "Oh, yes," and slowly searched in my mind for some more fitting acknowledgment of the compliment that his memory had paid me.

I was greatly astonished when he said, "You were wrong about the gnousar sickness; it was not that at all."

I said, "Why! Have you been there?"

And he said, "Yes; I do it with hashish. I know Bethmoora well." And he took out of his pocket a small box full of some black stuff that looked like tar, but had a stranger smell. He warned me not to touch it with my finger, as the stain remained for days. "I got it from a gipsy," he said. "He had a lot of it, as it had killed his father." But I interrupted him, for I wanted to know for certain what it was that had made desolate that beautiful city, Bethmoora, and why they fled from it swiftly in a day.

"Was it because of the Desert's curse?" I asked.

And he said, "Partly it was the fury of the Desert and partly the advice of the Emperor Thuba Mleen, for that fearful beast is in some way connected with the Desert on his mother's side." And he told me this strange story: "You remember the sailor with the black scar, who was there on the day that you described when the messengers came on mules to the gate of Bethmoora, and all the people fled. I met this man in a tavern, drinking rum, and he told me all about the flight from Bethmoora, but knew no more than you did what the message was, or who had sent it. However, he said he would see Bethmoora once more whenever he touched again at an eastern port, even if he had to face the Devil. He often said that he would face the Devil to find out the mystery of that message that emptied Bethmoora in a day. And in the end he had to face Thuba Mleen, whose weak ferocity he had not imagined. For one day the sailor told me he had found a ship, and I met him no more after that in the tavern drinking rum. It was about that time that I got the hashish from the gipsy, who had a quantity that he did not want. It takes one literally out of oneself. It is like wings. You swoop over distant countries and into other worlds. Once I found out the secret of the universe. I have forgotten what it was, but I know that the Creator does not take Creation seriously, for I remember that He sat in Space with all His work in front of Him and laughed. I have seen incredible things in fearful worlds. As it is your imagination that takes you there, so it is only by your imagination that you can get back. Once out in aether I met a battered, prowling spirit, that had belonged to a man whom drugs had killed a hundred years ago; and he led me to regions that I had never imagined; and we parted in anger beyond the Pleiades, and I could not imagine my way back. And I met a huge grey shape that was the Spirit of some great people, perhaps of a whole star, and I besought It to show me my way home, and It halted beside me like a sudden wind and pointed, and, speaking quite softly, asked me if I discerned a certain tiny light, and I saw a far star faintly, and then It said to me, 'That is the Solar System,' and strode tremendously on. And somehow I imagined my way back, and only just in time, for my body was already stiffening in a chair in my room; and the fire had gone out and everything was cold, and I had to move each finger one by one, and there were pins and needles in them, and dreadful pains in the nails, which began to thaw; and at last I could move one arm, and reached a bell, and for a long time no one came, because everyone was in bed. But at last a man appeared, and they got a doctor; and he said that it was hashish poisoning, but it would have been all right if I hadn't met that battered, prowling spirit.

"I could tell you astounding things that I have seen, but you want to know who sent that message to Bethmoora. Well, it was Thuba Mleen. And this is how I know. I often went to the city after that day you wrote of (I used to take hashish of an evening in my flat), and I always found it uninhabited. Sand had poured into it from the desert, and the streets were yellow and smooth, and through open, swinging doors the sand had drifted.

"One evening I had put the guard in front of the fire, and settled into a chair and eaten my hashish, and the first thing that I saw when I came to Bethmoora was the sailor with the black scar, strolling down the street, and making footprints in the yellow sand. And now I knew that I should see what secret power it was that kept Bethmoora uninhabited.

"I saw that there was anger in the Desert, for there were storm clouds heaving along the skyline, and I heard a muttering amongst the sand.

"The sailor strolled on down the street, looking into the empty houses as he went; sometimes he shouted and sometimes he sang, and sometimes he wrote his name on a marble wall. Then he sat down on a step and ate his dinner. After a while he grew tired of the city, and came back up the street. As he reached the gate of green copper three men on camels appeared.

"I could do nothing. I was only a consciousness, invisible, wandering: my body was in Europe. The sailor fought well with his fists, but he was over-powered and bound with ropes, and led away through the Desert.

"I followed for as long as I could stay, and found that they were going by the way of the Desert round the Hills of Hap towards Utnar Vehi, and then I knew that the camel men belonged to Thuba Mleen.

"I work in an insurance office all day, and I hope you won't forget me if ever you want to insure — life, fire, or motor — but that's no part of my story. I was desperately anxious to get back to my flat, though it is not good to take hashish two days running; but I wanted to see what they would do to the poor fellow, for I had heard bad rumours about Thuba Mleen. When at last I got away I had a letter to write; then I rang for my servant, and told him that I must not be disturbed, though I left my door unlocked in case of accidents. After that I made up a good fire, and sat down and partook of the pot of dreams. I was going to the palace of Thuba Mleen.

"I was kept back longer than usual by noises in the street, but suddenly I was up above the town; the European countries rushed by beneath me, and there appeared the thin white palace spires of horrible Thuba Mleen. I found him presently at the end of a little narrow room. A curtain of red leather hung behind him, on which all the names of God, written in Yannish, were worked with a golden thread. Three windows were small and high. The Emperor seemed no more than about twenty, and looked small and weak. No smiles came on his nasty yellow face, though he tittered continually. As I looked from his low forehead to his quivering underlip, I became aware that there was some horror about him, though I was not able to perceive what it was. And then I saw it — the man never blinked; and though later on I watched those eyes for a blink, it never happened once.

"And then I followed the Emperor's rapt glance, and I saw the sailor lying on the floor, alive but hideously rent, and the royal torturers were at work all round him. They had torn long strips from him, but had not detached them, and they were torturing the ends of them far away from the sailor."

The man that I met at dinner told me many things which I must omit.

"The sailor was groaning softly, and every time he groaned Thuba

Mleen tittered. I had no sense of smell, but I could hear and see, and I do not know which was the most revolting — the terrible condition of the sailor or the happy unblinking face of horrible Thuba Mleen.

"I wanted to go away, but the time was not yet come, and I had to stay where I was.

"Suddenly the Emperor's face began to twitch violently and his under lip quivered faster, and he whimpered with anger, and cried with a shrill voice, in Yannish, to the captain of his torturers that there was a spirit in the room. I feared not, for living men cannot lay hands on a spirit, but all the torturers were appalled at his anger, and stopped their work, for their hands trembled in fear. Then two men of the spear-guard slipped from the room, and each of them brought back presently a golden bowl, with knobs on it, full of hashish; and the bowls were large enough for heads to have floated in had they been filled with blood. And the two men fell to rapidly, each eating with two great spoons — there was enough in each spoonful to have given dreams to a hundred men. And there came upon them soon the hashish state, and their spirits hovered, preparing to go free, while I feared horribly, but ever and anon they fell back again to their bodies, recalled by some noise in the room. Still the men ate, but lazily now, and without ferocity. At last the great spoons dropped out of their hands, and their spirits rose and left them. I could not flee. And the spirits were more horrible than the men, because they were young men, and not yet wholly moulded to fit their fearful souls. Still the sailor groaned softly, evoking little titters from the Emperor Thuba Mleen. Then the two spirits rushed at me, and swept me thence as gusts of wind sweep butterflies, and away we went from that small, pale, heinous man. There was no escaping from these spirits' fierce insistence. The energy in my minute lump of the drug was overwhelmed by the huge spoonsful that these men had eaten with both hands. I was whirled over Arvle Woondery, and brought to the lands of Snith, and swept on still until I came to Kragua, and beyond this to those bleak lands that are nearly unknown to fancy. And we came at last to those ivory hills that are named the Mountains of Madness, and I tried to struggle against the spirits of that frightful Emperor's men, for I heard on the other side of the ivory hills the pittering of those beasts that prey on the mad, as they prowled up and down. It was no fault of mine that my little lump of hashish could not fight with their horrible spoonsful..."

Some one was tugging at the hall-door bell. Presently a servant came and told our host that a policeman in the hall wished to speak to him at once. He apologised to us, and went outside, and we heard a man in heavy boots, who spoke in a low voice to him. My friend got up and walked over to the window, and opened it, and looked outside. "I should think it will be a fine night," he said. Then he jumped out. When we put our astonished heads out of the window to look for him, he was already out of sight.

How the Enemy Came to Thlunrana

It had been prophesied of old and foreseen from the ancient days that its enemy would come to Thlunrana. And the date of its doom was known and the gate by which it would enter, yet none had prophesied of the enemy who he was save that he was of the gods though he dwelt with men. Meanwhile Thlunrana, that secret lamaserai, that chief cathedral of wizardry, was the terror of the valley in which it stood and of all lands round about it. So narrow and high were the windows and so strange when lighted at night that they seemed to regard men with the demoniac leer of something that had a secret in the dark. Who were the magicians and the deputy-magicians and the great arch-wizard of that furtive place nobody knew, for they went veiled in black and hooded and cloaked completely in black.

Though her doom was close upon her and the enemy of prophecy should come that very night through the open, southward door that was named the Gate of the Doom, yet that rocky edifice Thlunrana remained mysterious still, venerable, terrible, dark, and dreadfully crowned with her doom. It was not often that anyone dared wander near to Thlunrana by night when the moan of the magicians invoking we know not Whom rose faintly from inner chambers, scaring the drifting bats: but on the last night of all the man from the black-thatched cottage by the five pine-trees came, because he would see Thlunrana once again before the enemy that was divine, but dwelt with men, should come against it and it should be no more. Up the dark valley he went like a bold man; but his fears were thick upon him; his bravery bore their weight but stooped a little beneath them. He went in at the southward gate that is named the Gate of Doom. He came into a dark hall, and up a marble stairway passed to see the last of Thlunrana. At the top a curtain of black velvet hung and he passed into a chamber heavily hung with curtains, with a gloom in it that was blacker than anything they could account for. In a sombre chamber beyond, seen through a vacant archway, magicians with lighted tapers plied their wizardry and whispered incantations. All the rats in the place were passing away, going whimpering down the stairway. The man from the black-thatched cottage passed through that second chamber: the magicians did not look at him and did not cease to whisper. He passed from them through heavy curtains still of black velvet and came into a chamber of black marble where nothing stirred.

Only one taper burned in the third chamber; there were no windows. On the smooth floor and underneath the smooth wall a silk pavilion stood with its curtains drawn close together: this was the holy of holies of that ominous place, its inner mystery. One on each side of it dark figures crouched, either of men or women or cloaked stone, or of beasts trained to be silent. When the awful stillness of the mystery was more than he could bear the man from the black-thatched cottage by the five pine-trees went up to the silk pavilion, and with a bold and nervous clutch of the hand drew one of the curtains aside, and saw the inner mystery, and laughed. And the prophecy was fulfilled, and Thlunrana was never more a terror to the valley, but the magicians passed away from their terrific halls and fled through the open fields wailing and beating their breasts, for laughter was the enemy that was doomed to come against Thlunrana through her southward gate (that was named the Gate of Doom), and it is of the gods but dwells with man.

In Zaccarath

"Come," said the King in sacred Zaccarath, "and let our prophets prophesy before us."

A far-seen jewel of light was the holy palace, a wonder to the nomads on the plains.

There was the King with all his underlords, and the lesser kings that did him vassalage, and there were all his queens with all their jewels upon them.

Who shall tell of the splendour in which they sat; of the thousand lights and the answering emeralds; of the dangerous beauty of that hoard of queens, or the flash of their laden necks?

There was a necklace there of rose-pink pearls beyond the art of the dreamer to imagine. Who shall tell of the amethyst chandeliers, where torches, soaked in rare Bhyrinian oils, burned and gave off a scent of blethany?

(This herb marvellous, which, growing near the summit of Mount Zaumnos, scents all the Zaumnian range, and is smelt far out on the Kepuscran plains, and even, when the wind is from the mountains, in the streets of the city of Ognoth. At night it closes its petals and is heard to breathe, and its breath is a swift poison. This it does even by day if the snows are disturbed about it. No plant of this has ever been captured alive by a hunter.)

Enough to say that when the dawn came up it appeared by contrast pallid and unlovely and stripped bare of all its glory, so that it hid itself with rolling clouds.

"Come," said the King, "let our prophets prophesy."

Then the heralds stepped through the ranks of the King's silk-clad warriors who lay oiled and scented upon velvet cloaks, with a pleasant breeze among them caused by the fans of slaves; even their casting-spears were set with jewels; through their ranks the heralds went with mincing steps, and came to the prophets, clad in brown and black, and one of them they brought and set him before the King. And the King looked at him and said, "Prophesy unto us."

And the prophet lifted his head, so that his beard came clear from his brown cloak, and the fans of the slaves that fanned the warriors wafted the tip of it a little awry. And he spake to the King, and spake thus:

"Woe unto thee, King, and woe unto Zaccarath. Woe unto thee, and woe unto thy women, for your fall shall be sore and soon. Already in Heaven the gods shun thy god: they know his doom and what is written of him: he sees oblivion before him like a mist. Thou hast aroused the hate of the mountaineers. They hate thee all along the crags of Droom. The evilness of thy days shall bring down the Zeedians on thee as the suns of springtide bring the avalanche down. They shall do unto Zaccarath as the avalanche doth unto the hamlets of the valley." When the queens chattered or tittered among themselves, he merely raised his voice and still spake on: "Woe to these walls and the carven things upon them. The hunter shall know the camping-places of the nomads by the marks of the camp-fires on the plain, but he shall not know the place of Zaccarath."

A few of the recumbent warriors turned their heads to glance at the prophet when he ceased. Far overhead the echoes of his voice hummed on awhile among the cedarn rafters.

"Is he not splendid?" said the King. And many of that assembly beat with their palms upon the polished floor in token of applause. Then the prophet was conducted back to his place at the far end of that mighty hall, and for a while musicians played on marvellous curved horns, while drums throbbed behind them hidden in a recess. The musicians were sitting cross-legged on the floor, all blowing their huge horns in the brilliant torchlight, but as the drums throbbed louder in the dark they arose and moved slowly nearer to the King. Louder and louder drummed the drums in the dark, and nearer and nearer moved the men with the horns, so that their music should not be drowned by the drums before it reached the King.

A marvellous scene it was when the tempestuous horns were halted before the King, and the drums in the dark were like the thunder of God; and the queens were nodding their heads in time to the music, with their diadems flashing like heavens of falling stars; and the warriors lifted their heads and shook, as they lifted them, the plumes of those golden birds which hunters wait for by the Liddian lakes, in a whole lifetime killing scarcely six, to make the crests that the warriors wore when they feasted in Zaccarath. Then the King shouted and the warriors sang — almost they remembered then old battle-chants. And, as they sang, the sound of the drums dwindled, and the musicians walked away backwards, and the drumming became fainter and fainter as they walked, and altogether ceased, and they blew no more on their fantastic horns. Then the assemblage beat on the floor with their palms. And afterwards the queens besought the King to send for another prophet. And the heralds brought a singer, and placed him before the King; and the singer was a young man with a harp. And he swept the strings of it, and when there was silence he sang of the iniquity of the King. And he foretold the onrush of the Zeedians, and the fall and the forgetting of Zaccarath, and the coming again of the desert to its own, and the playing about of little lion cubs where the courts of the palace had stood.

"Of what is he singing?" said a queen to a queen.

"He is singing of everlasting Zaccarath."

As the singer ceased the assemblage beat listlessly on the floor, and the King nodded to him, and he departed.

When all the prophets had prophesied to them and all the singers sung, that royal company arose and went to other chambers, leaving the hall of festival to the pale and lonely dawn. And alone were left the lion-headed gods that were carven out of the walls; silent they stood, and their rocky arms were folded. And shadows over their faces moved like curious thoughts as the torches flickered and the dull dawn crossed the fields. And the colours began to change in the chandeliers.

When the last lutanist fell asleep the birds began to sing.

Never was greater splendour or a more famous hall. When the queens went away through the curtained door with all their diadems, it was as though the stars should arise in their stations and troop together to the West at sunrise.

And only the other day I found a stone that had undoubtedly been a part of Zaccarath, it was three inches long and an inch broad; I saw the edge of it uncovered by the sand. I believe that only three other pieces have been found like it.

The Idle City

There was once a city which was an idle city, wherein men told vain tales.

And it was that city's custom to tax all men that would enter in, with the toll of some idle story in the gate.

So all men paid to the watchers in the gate the toll of an idle story, and passed into the city unhindered and unhurt. And in a certain hour of the night when the king of that city arose and went pacing swiftly up and down the chamber of his sleeping, and called upon the name of the dead queen, then would the watchers fasten up the gate and go into that chamber to the king, and, sitting on the floor, would tell him all the tales that they had gathered.

And listening to them some calmer mood would come upon the king, and listening still he would lie down again and at last fall asleep, and all the watchers silently would arise and steal away from the chamber.

A while ago wandering, I came to the gate of that city.

And even as I came a man stood up to pay his toll to the watchers. They were seated cross-legged on the ground between him and the gate, and each one held a spear. Near him two other travellers sat on the warm sand waiting. And the man said:

"Now the city of Nombros forsook the worship of the gods and turned towards God. So the gods threw their cloaks over their faces and strode away from the city, and going into the haze among the hills passed through the trunks of the olive groves into the sunset. But when they had already left the earth, they turned and looked through the gleaming folds of the twilight for the last time at their city; and they looked half in anger and half in regret, then turned and went away for ever. But they sent back a Death, who bore a scythe, saying to it: 'Slay half in the city that forsook us, but half of them spare alive that they may yet remember their old forsaken gods.'

"But God sent a destroying angel to show that He was God, saying unto him: 'Go down and show the strength of mine arm unto that city and slay half of the dwellers therein, yet spare a half of them that they may know that I am God.'

"And at once the destroying angel put his hand to his sword, and the sword came out of the scabbard with a deep breath, like to the breath that a broad woodman takes before his first blow at some giant oak. Thereat the angel pointed his arms downwards, and bending his head between them, fell forward from Heaven's edge, and the spring of his ankles shot him downwards with his wings furled behind him. So he went slanting earthward through the evening with his sword stretched out before him, and he was like a javelin that some hunter hath hurled that returneth again to the earth: but just before he touched it he lifted his head and spread his wings with the under feathers forward, and alighted by the bank of the broad Flavro that divides the city of Nombros. And down the bank of the Flavro he fluttered low, like to a hawk over a new-cut cornfield when the little creatures of the corn are shelterless, and at the same time down the other bank the Death from the gods went mowing.

"At once they saw each other, and the angel glared at the Death, and the Death leered back at him, and the flames in the eyes of the angel illumined with a red glare the mist that lay in the hollows of the sockets of the Death. Suddenly they fell on one another, sword to scythe. And the angel captured the temples of the gods, and set up over them the sign of

God, and the Death captured the temples of God, and led into them the ceremonies and sacrifices of the gods; and all the while the centuries slipped quietly by going down the Flavro seawards.

"And now some worship God in the temple of the gods, and others worship the gods in the temple of God, and still the angel hath not returned again to the rejoicing choirs, and still the Death hath not gone back to die with the dead gods; but all through Nombros they fight up and down, and still on each side of the Flavro the city lives."

And the watchers in the gate said, "Enter in."

Then another traveller rose up, and said:

"Solemnly between Huhenwazi and Nitcrana the huge grey clouds came floating. And those great mountains, heavenly Huhenwazi, and Nitcrana, the king of peaks, greeted them, calling them brothers. And the clouds were glad of their greeting for they meet with companions seldom in the lonely heights of the sky.

"But the vapours of evening said unto the earth-mist, 'What are those shapes that dare to move above us and to go where Nitcrana is and Huhenwazi?'

"And the earth-mist said in answer unto the vapours of evening, 'It is only an earth-mist that has become mad and has left the warm and comfortable earth, and has in his madness thought that his place is with Huhenwazi and Nitcrana.'

" 'Once,' said the vapours of evening, 'there were clouds, but this was many and many a day ago, as our forefathers have said. Perhaps the mad one thinks he is the clouds.'

"Then spake the earth-worms from the warm deeps of the mud, saying 'O, earth-mist, thou art indeed the clouds, and there are no clouds but thou. And as for Huhenwazi and Nitcrana, I cannot see them, and therefore they are not high, and there are no mountains in the world but those that I cast up every morning out of the deeps of the mud.'

"And the earth-mist and the vapours of evening were glad at the voice of the earth-worms, and looking earthward believed what they had said.

"And indeed it is better to be as the earth-mist, and to keep close to the warm mud at night, and to hear the earth-worm's comfortable speech, and not to be a wanderer in the cheerless heights, but to leave the mountains alone with their desolate snow, to draw what comfort they can from their vast aspect over all the cities of men, and from the whispers that they hear at evening of unknown distant Gods."

And the watchers in the gate said, "Enter in."

Then a man stood up who came out of the west, and told a western tale. He said:

"There is a road in Rome that runs through an ancient temple that once the gods had loved; it runs along the top of a great wall, and the floor of the temple lies far down beneath it, of marble, pink and white.

"Upon the temple floor I counted to the number of thirteen hungry cats.

" 'Sometimes,' they said among themselves, 'It was the gods that lived here, sometimes it was men, and now it's cats. So let us enjoy the sun on the hot marble before another people comes.'

"For it was at that hour of a warm afternoon when my fancy is able to hear the silent voices.

"And the fearful leanness of all those thirteen cats moved me to go into a neighbouring fish shop, and there to buy a quantity of fishes. Then I returned and threw them all over the railing at the top of the great wall, and they fell for thirty feet, and hit the sacred marble with a smack.

"Now, in any other town but Rome, or in the minds of any other cats, the sight of fishes falling out of heaven had surely excited wonder. They rose slowly, and all stretched themselves, then they came leisurely towards the fishes. 'It is only a miracle,' they said in their hearts."

And the watchers in the gate said, "Enter in."

Proudly and slowly, as they spoke, drew up to them a camel, whose rider sought for entrance to the city. His face shone with the sunset by which for long he had steered for the city's gate. Of him they demanded toll. Whereat he spoke to his camel, and the camel roared and kneeled, and the man descended from him. And the man unwrapped from many silks a box of divers metals wrought by the Japanese, and on the lid of it were figures of men who gazed from some shore at an isle of the Inland Sea. This he showed to the watchers, and when they had seen it, said, "It has seemed to me that these speak to each other thus:

"Behold now Oojni, the dear one of the sea, the little mother sea that hath no storms. She goeth out from Oojni singing a song, and she returneth singing over her sands. Little is Oojni in the lap of the sea, and scarce to be perceived by wondering ships. White sails have never wafted her legends afar, they are told not by bearded wanderers of the sea. Her fireside tales are known not to the North, the dragons of China have not heard of them, nor those that ride on elephants through Ind.

"Men tell the tales and the smoke ariseth upwards; the smoke departeth and the tales are told.

"Oojni is not a name among the nations, she is not known of where the merchants meet, she is not spoken of by alien lips.

"Indeed, but Oojni is little among the isles, yet is she loved by those that know her coasts and her inland places hidden from the sea.

"Without glory, without fame, and without wealth, Oojni is greatly loved by a little people, and by a few; yet not by few, for all her dead still love her, and oft by night come whispering through her woods. Who could forget Oojni even among the dead?

"For here in Oojni, wot you, are homes of men, and gardens, and golden temples of the gods, and sacred places inshore from the sea, and many murmurous woods. And there is a path that winds over the hills to go into mysterious holy lands where dance by night the spirits of the woods, or sing unseen in the sunlight; and no one goes into these holy lands, for who that love Oojni would rob her of her mysteries, and the curious aliens come not. Indeed, but we love Oojni though she is so little; she is the little mother of our race, and the kindly nurse of all seafaring birds.

"And behold, even now caressing her, the gentle fingers of the mother sea, whose dreams are afar with that old wanderer Ocean.

"And yet let us forget not Fuzi-Yama, for he stands manifest over clouds and sea, misty below, and vague and indistinct, but clear above for all the isles to watch. The ships make all their journeys in his sight, the nights and the days go by him like a wind, the summers and winters under him flicker and fade, the lives of men pass quietly here and hence, and Fuzi-Yama watches there — and knows."

And the watchers in the gate said "Enter in."

And I too would have told them a tale, very wonderful and very true; one that I had told in many cities, which as yet had no believers. But now the sun had set, and the brief twilight gone, and ghostly silences were rising from far and darkening hills. A stillness hung over that city's gate. And the great silence of the solemn night was more acceptable to the watchers in the gate than any sound of man. Therefore they beckoned to us, and motioned with their hands that we should pass untaxed into the city. And softly we went up over the sand, and between the high rock pillars of the gate, and a deep stillness settled among the watchers, and the stars over them twinkled undisturbed.

For how short a while man speaks, and withal how vainly.

And for how long he is silent. Only the other day I met a king in Thebes, who had been silent already for four thousand years.

The Madness of Andelsprutz

I first saw the city of Andelsprutz on an afternoon in spring. The day was full of sunshine as I came by the way of the fields, and all that morning I had said, "There will be sunlight on it when I see for the first time the beautiful conquered city whose fame has so often made for me lovely dreams." Suddenly I saw its fortifications lifting out of the fields, and behind them stood its belfries. I went in by a gate and saw its houses and streets, and a great disappointment came upon me. For there is an air about a city, and it has a way with it, whereby a man may recognize one from another at once. There are cities full of happiness and cities full of pleasure, and cities full of gloom. There are cities with their faces to heaven, and some with their faces to earth; some have a way of looking at the past and others look at the future; some notice you if you come among them, others glance at you, others let you go by. Some love the cities that are their neighbours, others are dear to the plains and to the heath; some cities are bare to the wind, others have purple cloaks and others brown cloaks, and some are clad in white. Some tell the old tale of their infancy, with others it is secret; some cities sing and some mutter, some are angry, and some have broken hearts, and each city has her way of greeting Time.

I had said: "I will see Andelsprutz arrogant with her beauty," and I had said: "I will see her weeping over her conquest."

I had said: "She will sing songs to me," and "she will be reticent," "she will be all robed," and "she will be bare but splendid."

But the windows of Andelsprutz in her houses looked vacantly over the plains like the eyes of a dead madman. At the hour her chimes sounded unlovely and discordant, some of them were out of tune, and the bells of some were cracked, her roofs were bald and without moss. At evening no pleasant rumour arose in her streets. When the lamps were lit in the houses no mystical flood of light stole out into the dusk, you merely saw that there were lighted lamps; Andelsprutz had no way with her and no air about her. When the night fell and the blinds were all drawn down, then I perceived what I had not thought in the daylight. I knew then that Andelsprutz was dead.

I saw a fair-haired man who drank beer in a cafe, and I said to him: "Why is the city of Andelsprutz quite dead, and her soul gone hence?"

He answered: "Cities do not have souls and there is never any life in bricks."

And I said to him: "Sir, you have spoken truly."

And I asked the same question of another man, and he gave me the same answer, and I thanked him for his courtesy. And I saw a man of a more slender build, who had black hair, and channels in his cheeks for tears to run in, and I said to him: "Why is Andelsprutz quite dead, and when did her soul go hence?"

And he answered: "Andelsprutz hoped too much. For thirty years would she stretch out her arms toward the land of Akla every night, to Mother Akla from whom she had been stolen. Every night she would be hoping and sighing, and stretching out her arms to Mother Akla. At midnight, once a year, on the anniversary of the terrible day, Akla would send spies to lay a wreath against the walls of Andelsprutz. She could do no more. And on this night, once in every year, I used to weep, for weeping was the mood of the city that nursed me. Every night while other cities slept did Andelsprutz sit brooding here and hoping, till thirty wreaths lay mouldering by her walls, and still the armies of Akla could not come.

"But after she had hoped so long, and on the night that faithful spies had brought the thirtieth wreath, Andelsprutz went suddenly mad. All the bells clanged hideously in the belfries, horses bolted in the streets, the dogs all howled, the stolid conquerors awoke and turned in their beds and slept again; and I saw the grey shadowy form of Andelsprutz rise up, decking her hair with the phantasms of cathedrals, and stride away from her city. And the great shadowy form that was the soul of Andelsprutz went away muttering to the mountains, and there I followed her — for had she not been my nurse? Yes, I went away alone into the mountains, and for three days, wrapped in a cloak, I slept in their misty solitudes. I had no food to eat, and to drink I had only the water of the mountain streams. By day no living thing was near to me, and I heard nothing but the noise of the wind, and the mountain streams roaring. But for three nights I heard all round me on the mountain the sounds of a great city: I saw the lights of tall cathedral windows flash momentarily on the peaks, and at times the glimmering lantern of some fortress patrol. And I saw the huge misty outline of the soul of Andelsprutz sitting decked with her ghostly cathedrals, speaking to herself, with her eyes fixed before her in a mad stare, telling of ancient wars. And in her confused speech for all those nights upon the mountain was sometimes the voice of traffic, and then of church bells, and then of the bugles, but oftenest it was the voice of red war; and it was all incoherent, and she was quite mad.

"The third night it rained heavily all night long, but I stayed up there to watch the soul of my native city. And she still sat staring straight before her, raving; but her voice was gentler now, there were more chimes in it, and occasional song. Midnight passed, and the rain still swept down on me, and still the solitudes of the mountain were full of the mutterings of the poor mad city. And the hours after midnight came, the cold hours wherein sick men die.

"Suddenly I was aware of great shapes moving in the rain, and heard the sound of voices that were not of my city nor yet of any that I ever knew. And presently I discerned, though faintly, the souls of a great concourse of cities, all bending over Andelsprutz and comforting her, and the ravines of the mountains roared that night with the voices of cities that had lain still for centuries. For there came the soul of Camelot that had so long ago forsaken Usk; and there was Ilion, all girt with towers, still cursing the sweet face of ruinous Helen; I saw there Babylon and Persepolis, and the bearded face of bull-like Nineveh, and Athens mourning her immortal gods.

"All these souls of cities that were dead spoke that night on the mountain to my city and soothed her, until at last she muttered of war no longer, and her eyes stared wildly no more, but she hid her face in her hands and for some while wept softly. At last she arose, and, walking slowly and with bended head, and leaning upon Ilion and Carthage, went mournfully eastwards; and the dust of her highways swirled behind her as she went, a ghostly dust that never turned to mud in all that drenching rain. And so the souls of the cities led her away, and gradually they disappeared from the mountain, and the ancient voices died away in the distance.

"Never since then have I seen my city alive; but once I met with a traveller who said that somewhere in the midst of a great desert are gathered together the souls of all dead cities. He said that he was lost once in a place where there was no water, and he heard their voices speaking all the night."

But I said: "I was once without water in a desert and heard a city speaking to me, but knew not whether it really spoke or not, for on that day I heard so many terrible things, and only some of them were true."

And the man with the black hair said: "I believe it to be true, though whither she went I know not. I only know that a shepherd found me in the morning faint with hunger and cold, and carried me down here; and when I came to Andelsprutz it was, as you have perceived it, dead."

The Secret of the Sea

In an ill-lit ancient tavern that I know, are many tales of the sea; but not without the wine of Gorgondy, that I had of a private bargain with the gnomes, was the tale laid bare for which I had waited of an evening for the greater part of a year.

I knew my man and listened to his stories, sitting amid the bluster of his oaths; I plied him with rum and whiskey and mixed drinks, but there never came the tale for which I sought, and as a last resort I went to the Huthneth Mountains and bargained there all night with the chief of the gnomes.

When I came to the ancient tavern and entered the low-roofed room, bringing the hoard of the gnomes in a bottle of hammered iron, my man had not yet arrived. The sailors laughed at my old iron bottle, but I sat down and waited; had I opened it then they would have wept and sung. I was well content to wait, for I knew my man had the story, and it was such a one as had profoundly stirred the incredulity of the faithless.

He entered and greeted me, and sat down and called for brandy. He was a hard man to turn from his purpose, and, uncorking my iron bottle, I sought to dissuade him from brandy for fear that when the brandy bit his throat he would refuse to leave it for any other wine. He lifted his head and said deep and dreadful things of any man that should dare to speak against brandy.

I swore that I had nothing against brandy but added that it was often given to children, while Gorgondy was only drunk by men of such depravity that they had abandoned sin because all the usual vices had come to seem genteel. When he asked if Gorgondy was a bad wine to drink I said that it was so bad that if a man sipped it that was the one touch that made damnation certain. Then he asked me what I had in the iron bottle, and I said it was Gorgondy; and then he shouted for the largest tumbler in that ill-lit ancient tavern, and stood up and shook his fist at me when it came, and swore, and told me to fill it with the wine that I got on that bitter night from the treasure house of the gnomes.

As he drank it he told me that he had met men who had spoken against wine, and that they had mentioned Heaven; and therefore he would not go there — no, not he; and that once he had sent one of them to Hell, but when he got there he would turn him out, and he had no use for milksops.

Over the second tumbler he was thoughtful, but still he said no word of the tale he knew, until I feared that it would never be heard. But when the third glass of that terrific wine had burned its way down his gullet, and vindicated the wickedness of the gnomes, his reticence withered like a leaf in the fire, and he bellowed out the secret.

I had long known that there is in ships a will or way of their own, and had even suspected that when sailors die or abandon their ships at sea, a derelict, being left to her own devices, may seek her own ends; but I had never dreamed by night, or fancied during the day, that the ships had a god that they worshipped, or that they secretly slipped away to a temple in the sea.

Over the fourth glass of the wine that the gnomes so sinfully brew but have kept so wisely from man, until the bargain that I had with their elders all through that autumn night, the sailor told me the story. I do not tell it as he told it to me because of the oaths that were in it; nor is it from delicacy that I refrain from writing these oaths verbatim, but merely because the horror they caused in me at the time troubles me still whenever I put them on paper, and I continue to shudder until I have blotted them out. Therefore, I tell the story in my own words, which, if they possess a certain decency that was not in the mouth of that sailor, unfortunately do not smack, as his did, of rum and blood and the sea.

You would take a ship to be a dead thing like a table, as dead as bits of iron and canvas and wood. That is because you always live on shore, and have never seen the sea, and drink milk. Milk is a more accursed drink than water.

What with the captain and what with the man at the wheel, and what with the crew, a ship has no fair chance of showing a will of her own.

There is only one moment in the history of ships, that carry crews on board, when they act by their own free will. This moment comes when all the crew are drunk. As the last man falls drunk on to the deck, the ship is free of man, and immediately slips away. She slips away at once on a new course and is never one yard out in a hundred miles.

It was like this one night with the Sea-Fancy. Bill Smiles was there himself, and can vouch for it. Bill Smiles has never told this tale before for fear that anyone should call him a liar. Nobody dislikes being hung as much as Bill Smiles would, but he won't be called a liar. I tell the tale as I heard it, relevancies and irrelevancies, though in my more decent words; and as I made no doubts of the truth of it then, I hardly like to now; others can please themselves.

It is not often that the whole of a crew is drunk. The crew of the Sea-Fancy was no drunkener than others. It happened like this.

The captain was always drunk. One day a fancy he had that some spiders were plotting against him, or a sudden bleeding he had from both his ears, made him think that drinking might be bad for his health. Next day he signed the pledge. He was sober all that morning and all the afternoon, but at evening he saw a sailor drinking a glass of beer, and a fit of madness seized him, and he said things that seemed bad to Bill Smiles. And next morning he made all of them take the pledge.

For two days nobody had a drop to drink, unless you count water, and on the third morning the captain was quite drunk. It stood to reason they all had a glass or two then, except the man at the wheel; and towards evening the man at the wheel could bear it no longer, and seems to have had his glass like all the rest, for the ship's course wobbled a bit and made a circle or two. Then all of a sudden she went off south by east under full canvas till midnight, and never altered her course. And at midnight she came to the wide wet courts of the Temple in the Sea.

People who think that Mr. Smiles is drunk often make a great mistake. And people are not the only ones that have made that mistake. Once a ship made it, and a lot of ships. It's a mistake to think that old Bill Smiles is drunk just because he can't move.

Midnight and moonlight and the Temple of the Sea Bill Smiles clearly remembers, and all the derelicts in the world were there, the old abandoned ships. The figureheads were nodding to themselves and blinking at the image. The image was a woman of white marble on a pedestal in the outer court of the Temple of the Sea: she was clearly the love of all the man-deserted ships, or the goddess to whom they prayed their heathen prayers. And as Bill Smiles was watching them, the lips of the figureheads moved; they all began to pray. But all at once their lips were closed with a snap when they saw that there were men on the Sea-Fancy. They all came crowding up and nodded and nodded and nodded to see if all were drunk, and that's when they made their mistake about old Bill Smiles, although he couldn't move. They would have given up the treasuries of the gulfs sooner than let men hear the prayers they said or guess their love for the goddess. It is the intimate secret of the sea.

The sailor paused. And, in my eagerness to hear what lyrical or blasphemous thing those figureheads prayed by moonlight at midnight in the sea to the woman of marble who was a goddess to ships, I pressed on the sailor more of my Gorgondy wine that the gnomes so wickedly brew.

I should never have done it; but there he was sitting silent while the secret was almost mine. He took it moodily and drank a glass; and with the other glasses that he had had he fell a prey to the villainy of the gnomes who brew this unbridled wine to no good end. His body leaned forward slowly, then fell on to the table, his face being sideways and full of a wicked smile, and, saying very clearly the one word, "Hell," he became silent for ever with the secret he had from the sea.

Idle Days on the Yann

So I came down through the wood to the bank of Yann and found, as had been prophesied, the ship Bird of the River about to loose her cable.

The captain sate cross-legged upon the white deck with his scimitar lying beside him in its jewelled scabbard, and the sailors toiled to spread the nimble sails to bring the ship into the central stream of Yann, and all the while sang ancient soothing songs. And the wind of the evening descending cool from the snowfields of some mountainous abode of distant gods came suddenly, like glad tidings to an anxious city, into the wing-like sails.

And so we came into the central stream, whereat the sailors lowered the greater sails. But I had gone to bow before the captain, and to inquire concerning the miracles, and appearances among men, of the most holy gods of whatever land he had come from. And the captain answered that he came from fair Belzoond, and worshipped gods that were the least and humblest, who seldom sent the famine or the thunder, and were easily appeased with little battles. And I told how I came from Ireland, which is of Europe, whereat the captain and all the sailors laughed, for they said, "There are no such places in all the land of dreams." When they had ceased to mock me, I explained that my fancy mostly dwelt in the desert of Cuppar-Nombo, about a beautiful blue city called Golthoth the Damned, which was sentinelled all round by wolves and their shadows, and had been utterly desolate for years and years, because of a curse which the gods once spoke in anger and could never since recall. And sometimes my dreams took me as far as Pungar Vees, the red walled city where the fountains are, which trades with the Isles and Thul. When I said this they complimented me upon the abode of my fancy, saying that, though they had never seen these cities, such places might well be imagined. For the rest of that evening I bargained with the captain over the sum that I should pay him for my fare if God and the tide of Yann should bring us safely as far as the cliffs by the sea, which are named Bar-Wul-Yann, the Gate of Yann.

And now the sun had set, and all the colors of the world and heaven had held a festival with him, and slipped one by one away before the imminent approach of night. The parrots had all flown home to the jungle on either bank, the monkeys in rows in safety on high branches of the trees were silent and asleep, the fireflies in the deeps of the forest were going up and down, and the great stars came gleaming out to look on the face of Yann. Then the sailors lighted lanterns and hung them round the ship, and the light flashed out on a sudden and dazzled Yann, and the ducks that fed along his marshy banks all suddenly arose, and made wide circles in the upper air, and saw the distant reaches of the Yann and the white mist that softly cloaked the jungle, before they returned again into their marshes.

And then the sailors knelt on the decks and prayed, not all together, but five or six at a time. Side by side there kneeled down together five or six, for there only prayed at the same time men of different faiths, so that no god should hear two men praying to him at once. As soon as any one had finished his prayer, another of the same faith would take his place. Thus knelt the row of five or six with bended heads under the fluttering sail, while the central stream of the River Yann took them on towards the sea, and their prayers rose up from among the lanterns and went towards the stars. And behind them in the after end of the ship the helmsman prayed aloud the helmsman's prayer, which is prayed by all who follow his trade upon the River Yann, of whatever faith they be. And the captain prayed to his little lesser gods, to the gods that bless Belzoond.

And I too felt that I would pray. Yet I liked not to pray to a jealous God there where the frail affectionate gods whom the heathen love were being humbly invoked; so I bethought me, instead, of Sheol Nugganoth, whom the men of the jungle have long since deserted, who is now unworshipped and alone; and to him I prayed.

And upon us praying the night came suddenly down, as it comes upon all men who pray at evening and upon all men who do not; yet our prayers comforted our own souls when we thought of the Great Night to come.

And so Yann bore us magnificently onwards, for he was elate with molten snow that the Poltiades had brought him from the Hills of Hap, and the Marn and Migris were swollen with floods; and he bore us in his full might past Kyph and Pir, and we saw the lights of Goolunza.

Soon we all slept except the helmsman, who kept the ship in the mid-stream of Yann.

When the sun rose the helmsman ceased to sing, for by song he cheered himself in the lonely night. When the song ceased we suddenly all awoke, and another took the helm, and the helmsman slept.

We knew that soon we should come to Mandaroon. We made a meal, and Mandaroon appeared. Then the captain commanded, and the sailors loosed again the greater sails, and the ship turned and left the stream of Yann and came into a harbour beneath the ruddy walls of Mandaroon. Then while the sailors went and gathered fruits I came alone to the gate of Mandaroon. A few huts were outside it, in which lived the guard. A sentinel with a long white beard was standing in the gate, armed with a rusty pike. He wore large spectacles, which were covered with dust. Through the gate I saw the city. A deathly stillness was over all of it. The ways seemed untrodden, and moss was thick on doorsteps; in the market-place huddled figures lay asleep. A scent of incense came wafted through the gateway, of incense and burned poppies, and there was a hum of the echoes of distant bells. I said to the sentinel in the tongue of the region of Yann, "Why are they all asleep in this still city?"

He answered: "None may ask questions in this gate for fear they will wake the people of the city. For when the people of this city wake the gods will die. And when the gods die men may dream no more." And I began to ask him what gods that city worshipped, but he lifted his pike because none might ask questions there. So I left him and went back to the Bird of the River.

Certainly Mandaroon was beautiful with her white pinnacles peering over her ruddy walls and the green of her copper roofs.

When I came back again to the Bird of the River, I found the sailors were returned to the ship. Soon we weighed anchor, and sailed out again, and so came once more to the middle of the river. And now the sun was moving toward his heights, and there had reached us on the River Yann the song of those countless myriads of choirs that attend him in his progress round the world. For the little creatures that have many legs had spread their gauze wings easily on the air, as a man rests his elbows on a balcony and gave jubilant, ceremonial praises to the sun, or else they moved together on the air in wavering dances intricate and swift, or turned aside to avoid the onrush of some drop of water that a breeze had shaken from a jungle orchid, chilling the air and driving it before it, as it fell whirring in its rush to the earth; but all the while they sang triumphantly. "For the day is for us," they said, "whether our great and sacred father the Sun shall bring up more life like us from the marshes, or whether all the world shall end to-night." And there sang all those whose notes are known to human ears, as well as those whose far more numerous notes have been never heard by man.

To these a rainy day had been as an era of war that should desolate continents during all the lifetime of a man.

And there came out also from the dark and steaming jungle to behold and rejoice in the Sun the huge and lazy butterflies. And they danced, but danced idly, on the ways of the air, as some haughty queen of distant conquered lands might in her poverty and exile dance, in some encampment of the gipsies, for the mere bread to live by, but beyond that would never abate her pride to dance for a fragment more.

And the butterflies sung of strange and painted things, of purple orchids and of lost pink cities and the monstrous colours of the jungle's decay. And they, too, were among those whose voices are not discernible by human ears. And as they floated above the river, going from forest to forest, their splendour was matched by the inimical beauty of the birds who darted out to pursue them. Or sometimes they settled on the white and wax-like blooms of the plant that creeps and clambers about the trees of the forest; and their purple wings flashed out on the great blossoms as, when the caravans go from Nurl to Thace, the gleaming silks flash out upon the snow, where the crafty merchants spread them one by one to astonish the mountaineers of the Hills of Noor.

But upon men and beasts the sun sent drowsiness. The river monsters along the river's marge lay dormant in the slime. The sailors pitched a pavillion, with golden tassels, for the captain upon the deck, and then went, all but the helmsman, under a sail that they had hung as an awning between two masts. Then they told tales to one another, each of his own city or of the miracles of his god, until all were fallen asleep. The captain offered me the shade of his pavillion with the gold tassels, and there we talked for awhile, he telling me that he was taking merchandise to Perdondaris, and that he would take back to fair Belzoond things appertaining to the affairs of the sea. Then, as I watched through the pavillion's opening the brilliant birds and butterflies that crossed and recrossed over the river, I fell asleep, and dreamed that I was a monarch entering his capital underneath arches of flags, and all the musicians of the world were there, playing melodiously their instruments; but no one cheered.

In the afternoon, as the day grew cooler again, I awoke and found the captain buckling on his scimitar, which he had taken off him while he rested.

And now we were approaching the wide court of Astahahn, which opens upon the river. Strange boats of antique design were chained there to the steps. As we neared it we saw the open marble court, on three sides of which stood the city fronting on colonnades. And in the court and along the colonnades the people of that city walked with solemnity and care according to the rites of ancient ceremony. All in that city was of ancient device; the carving on the houses, which, when age had broken it, remained unrepaired, was of the remotest times, and everywhere were represented in stone beasts that have long since passed away from Earth — the dragon, the griffin, the hippogriffin, and the different species of gargoyle. Nothing was to be found, whether material or custom, that was new in Astahahn. Now they took no notice at all of us as we went by, but continued their processions and ceremonies in the ancient city, and the sailors, knowing their custom, took no notice of them. But I called, as we came near, to one who stood beside the water's edge, asking him what men did in Astahahn and what their merchandise was, and with whom they traded. He said, "Here we have fettered and manacled Time, who would otherwise slay the gods."

I asked him what gods they worshipped in that city, and he said, "All those gods whom Time has not yet slain." Then he turned from me and would say no more, but busied himself in behaving in accordance with ancient custom. And so, according to the will of Yann, we drifted onwards and left Astahahn. The river widened below Astahahn, and we found in greater quantities such birds as prey on fishes. And they were very wonderful in their plumage, and they came not out of the jungle, but flew, with their long necks stretched out before them, and their legs lying on the wind behind, straight up the river over the mid-stream.

And now the evening began to gather in. A thick white mist had appeared over the river, and was softly rising higher. It clutched at the trees with long impalpable arms, it rose higher and higher, chilling the air; and white shapes moved away into the jungle as though the ghosts of shipwrecked mariners were searching stealthily in the darkness for the spirits of evil that long ago had wrecked them on the Yann.

As the sun sank behind the field of orchids that grew on the matted summit of the jungle, the river monsters came wallowing out of the slime in which they had reclined during the heat of the day, and the great beasts of the jungle came down to drink. The butterflies a while since were gone to rest. In little narrow tributaries that we passed night seemed already to have fallen, though the sun which had disappeared from us had not yet set.

And now the birds of the jungle came flying home far over us, with the sunlight glistening pink upon their breasts, and lowered their pinions as soon as they saw the Yann, and dropped into the trees. And the widgeon began to go up the river in great companies, all whistling, and then would suddenly wheel and all go down again. And there shot by us the small and arrow-like teal; and we heard the manifold cries of flocks of geese, which the sailors told me had recently come in from crossing over the Lispasian ranges; every year they come by the same way, close by the peak of Mluna, leaving it to the left, and the mountain eagles know the way they come and — men say — the very hour, and every year they expect them by the same way as soon as the snows have fallen upon the Northern Plains. But soon it grew so dark that we heard those birds no more, and only heard the whirring of their wings, and of countless others besides, until they all settled down along the banks of the river, and it was the hour when the birds of the night went forth. Then the sailors lit the lanterns for the night, and huge moths appeared, flapping about the ship, and at moments their gorgeous colours would be revealed by the lanterns, then they would pass into the night again, where all was black. And again the sailors prayed, and thereafter we supped and slept, and the helmsman took our lives into his care.

When I awoke I found that we had indeed come to Perdondaris, that famous city. For there it stood upon the left of us, a city fair and notable, and all the more pleasant for our eyes to see after the jungle that was so long with us. And we were anchored by the market-place, and the captain's merchandise was all displayed, and a merchant of Perdondaris stood looking at it. And the captain had his scimitar in his hand, and was beating with it in anger upon the deck, and the splinters were flying up from the white planks; for the merchant had offered him a price for his merchandise that the captain declared to be an insult to himself and his country's gods, whom he now said to be great and terrible gods, whose curses were to be dreaded. But the merchant waved his hands, which were of great fatness, showing the pink palms, and swore that of himself he thought not at all, but only of the poor folk in the huts beyond the city to whom he wished to sell the merchandise for as low a price as possible, leaving no remuneration for himself. For the merchandise was mostly the thick toomarund carpets that in the winter keep the wind from the floor, and tollub which the people smoke in pipes. Therefore the merchant said if he offered a piffek more the poor folk must go without their toomarunds when the winter came, and without their tollub in the evenings, or else he and his aged father must starve together. Thereat the captain lifted his scimitar to his own throat, saying that he was now a ruined man, and that nothing remained to him but death. And while he was carefully lifting his beard with his left hand, the merchant eyed the merchandise again, and said that rather than see so worthy a captain die, a man for whom he had conceived an especial love when first he saw the manner in which he handled his ship, he and his aged father should starve together and therefore he offered fifteen piffeks more.

When he said this the captain prostrated himself and prayed to his gods that they might yet sweeten this merchant's bitter heart — to his little lesser gods, to the gods that bless Belzoond.

At last the merchant offered yet five piffeks more. Then the captain wept, for he said that he was deserted of his gods; and the merchant also wept, for he said that he was thinking of his aged father, and of how he soon would starve, and he hid his weeping face with both his hands, and eyed the tollub again between his fingers. And so the bargain was concluded, and the merchant took the toomarund and tollub, paying for them out of a great clinking purse. And these were packed up into bales again, and three of the merchant's slaves carried them upon their heads into the city. And all the while the sailors had sat silent, cross-legged in a crescent upon the deck, eagerly watching the bargain, and now a murmur of satisfaction arose among them, and they began to compare it among themselves with other bargains that they had known. And I found out from them that there are seven merchants in Perdondaris, and that they had all come to the captain one by one before the bargaining began, and each had warned him privately against the others. And to all the merchants the captain had offered the wine of his own country, that they make in fair Belzoond, but could in no wise persuade them to it. But now that the bargain was over, and the sailors were seated at the first meal of the day, the captain appeared among them with a cask of that wine, and we broached it with care and all made merry together. And the captain was glad in his heart because he knew that he had much honour in the eyes of his men because of the bargain that he had made. So the sailors drank the wine of their native land, and soon their thoughts were back in fair Belzoond and the little neighbouring cities of Durl and Duz.

But for me the captain poured into a little jar some heavy yellow wine from a small jar which he kept apart among his sacred things. Thick and sweet it was, even like honey, yet there was in its heart a mighty, ardent fire which had authority over souls of men. It was made, the captain told me, with great subtlety by the secret craft of a family of six who lived in a hut on the mountains of Hian Min. Once in these mountains, he said, he followed the spoor of a bear, and he came suddenly on a man of that family who had hunted the same bear, and he was at the end of a narrow way with precipice all about him, and his spear was sticking in the bear, and the wound was not fatal, and he had no other weapon. And the bear was walking towards the man, very slowly because his wound irked him — yet he was now very close. And what he captain did he would not say, but every year as soon as the snows are hard, and travelling is easy on the Hian Min, that man comes down to the market in the plains, and always leaves for the captain in the gate of fair Belzoond a vessel of that priceless secret wine.

And as I sipped the wine and the captain talked, I remembered me of stalwart noble things that I had long since resolutely planned, and my soul seemed to grow mightier within me and to dominate the whole tide of the Yann. It may be that I then slept. Or, if I did not, I do not now minutely recollect every detail of that morning's occupations. Towards evening, I awoke and wishing to see Perdondaris before we left in the morning, and being unable to wake the captain, I went ashore alone. Certainly Perdondaris was a powerful city; it was encompassed by a wall of great strength and altitude, having in it hollow ways for troops to walk in, and battlements along it all the way, and fifteen strong towers on it in every mile, and copper plaques low down where men could read them, telling in all the languages of those parts of the earth — one language on each plaque — the tale of how an army once attacked Perdondaris and what befell that army. Then I entered Perdondaris and found all the people dancing, clad in brilliant silks, and playing on the tambang as they danced. For a fearful thunderstorm had terrified them while I slept, and the fires of death, they said, had danced over Perdondaris, and now the thunder had gone leaping away large and black and hideous, they said, over the distant hills, and had turned round snarling at them, shoving his gleaming teeth, and had stamped, as he went, upon the hilltops until they rang as though they had been bronze. And often and again they stopped in their merry dances and prayed to the God they knew not, saying, "O, God that we know not, we thank Thee for sending the thunder back to his hills." And I went on and came to the market-place, and lying there upon the marble pavement I saw the merchant fast asleep and breathing heavily, with his face and the palms of his hands towards the sky, and slaves were fanning him to keep away the flies. And from the market-place I came to a silver temple and then to a palace of onyx, and there were many wonders in Perdondaris, and I would have stayed and seen them all, but as I came to the outer wall of the city I suddenly saw in it a huge ivory gate. For a while I paused and admired it, then I came nearer and perceived the dreadful truth. The gate was carved out of one solid piece!

I fled at once through the gateway and down to the ship, and even as I ran I thought that I heard far off on the hills behind me the tramp of the fearful beast by whom that mass of ivory was shed, who was perhaps even then looking for his other tusk. When I was on the ship again I felt safer, and I said nothing to the sailors of what I had seen.

And now the captain was gradually awakening. Now night was rolling up from the East and North, and only the pinnacles of the towers of Perdondaris still took the fallen sunlight. Then I went to the captain and told him quietly of the thing I had seen. And he questioned me at once about the gate, in a low voice, that the sailors might not know; and I told him how the weight of the thing was such that it could not have been brought from afar, and the captain knew that it had not been there a year ago. We agreed that such a beast could never have been killed by any assault of man, and that the gate must have been a fallen tusk, and one fallen near and recently. Therefore he decided that it were better to flee at once; so he commanded, and the sailors went to the sails, and others raised the anchor to the deck, and just as the highest pinnacle of marble lost the last rays of the sun we left Perdondaris, that famous city. And night came down and cloaked Perdondaris and hid it from our eyes, which as things have happened will never see it again; for I have heard since that something swift and wonderful has suddenly wrecked Perdondaris in a day — towers, walls and people.

And the night deepened over the River Yann, a night all white with stars. And with the night there rose the helmsman's song. As soon as he had prayed he began to sing to cheer himself all through the lonely night. But first he prayed, praying the helmsman's prayer. And this is what I remember of it, rendered into English with a very feeble equivalent of the rhythm that seemed so resonant in those tropic nights.

To whatever god may hear.

Wherever there be sailors whether of river or sea: whether their way be dark or whether through storm: whether their peril be of beast or of rock: or from enemy lurking on land or pursuing on sea: wherever the tiller is cold or the helmsman stiff: wherever sailors sleep or helmsmen watch: guard, guide and return us to the old land, that has known us: to the far homes that we know.

To all the gods that are.

To whatever god may hear.

So he prayed, and there was silence. And the sailors laid them down to rest for the night. The silence deepened, and was only broken by the ripples of Yann that lightly touched our prow. Sometimes some monster of the river coughed.

Silence and ripples, ripples and silence again.

And then his loneliness came upon the helmsman, and he began to sing. And he sang the market songs of Durl and Duz, and the old dragon-legends of Belzoond.

Many a song he sang, telling to spacious and exotic Yann the little tales and trifles of his city of Durl. And the songs welled up over the black jungle and came into the clear cold air above, and the great bands of stars that look on Yann began to know the affairs of Durl and Duz, and of the shepherds that dwelt in the fields between, and the flocks that they had, and the loves that they had loved, and all the little things that they had hoped to do. And as I lay wrapped up in skins and blankets, listening to those songs, and watching the fantastic shapes of the great trees like to black giants stalking through the night, I suddenly fell asleep.

When I awoke great mists were trailing away from the and little waves appeared; for Yann had scented from afar the ancient crags of Glorm, and knew that their ravines lay cool before him wherein he should meet the merry wild Irillion rejoicing from fields of snow. So he shook off from him the torpid sleep that had come upon him in the hot and scented jungle, and forgot its orchids and its butterflies, and swept on turbulent, expectant, strong; and soon the snowy peaks of the Hills of Glorm came glittering into view. And now the sailors were waking up from sleep. Soon we all ate, and then the helmsman laid him down to sleep while a comrade took his place, and they all spread over him their choicest furs.

And in a while we heard the sound that the Irillion made as she came down dancing from the fields of snow.

And then we saw the ravine in the Hills of Glorm lying precipitous and smooth before us, into which we were carried by the leaps of Yann. And now we left the steamy jungle and breathed the mountain air; the sailors stood up and took deep breaths of it, and thought of their own far-off Acroctian hills on which were Durl and Duz — below them in the plains stands fair Belzoond.

A great shadow brooded between the cliffs of Glorm, but the crags were shining above us like gnarled moons, and almost lit the gloom. Louder and louder came the Irillion's song, and the sound of her dancing down from the fields of snow. And soon we saw her white and full of mists, and wreathed with rainbows delicate and small that she had plucked up near the mountain's summit from some celestial garden of the Sun. Then she went away seawards with the huge grey Yann and the ravine widened, and opened upon the world, and our rocking ship came through to the light of the day.

And all that morning and all the afternoon we passed through the marshes of Pondoovery; and Yann widened there, and flowed solemnly and slowly, and the captain bade the sailors beat on bells to overcome the dreariness of the marshes.

At last the Irusian mountains came in sight, nursing the villages of Pen-Kai and Blut, and the wandering streets of Mlo, where priests propitiate the avalanche with wine and maize. Then night came down over the plains of Tlun, and we saw the lights of Cappadarnia. We heard the Pathnites beating upon drums as we passed Imaut and Golzunda, then all but the helmsman slept. And villages scattered along the banks of the Yann heard all that night in the helmsman's unknown tongue the little songs of cities that they knew not.

I awoke before dawn with a feeling that I was unhappy before I remembered why. Then I recalled that by the evening of the approaching day, according to all foreseen probabilities, we should come to Bar-Wul-Yann, and I should part from the captain and his sailors. And I had liked the man because he had given me of his yellow wine that was set apart among his sacred things, and many a story he had told me about his fair Belzoond between the Acroctian hills and the Hian Min. And I had liked the ways that his sailors had, and the prayers that they prayed at evening side by side, grudging not one another their alien gods. And I had a liking too for the tender way in which they often spoke of Durl and Duz, for it is good that men should love their native cities and the little hills that hold those cities up.

And I had come to know who would meet them when they returned to their homes, and where they thought the meetings would take place, some in a valley of the Acroctian hills where the road comes up from Yann, others in the gateway of one or another of the three cities, and others by the fireside in the home. And I thought of the danger that had menaced us all alike outside Perdondaris, a danger that, as things have happened, was very real.

And I thought too of the helmsman's cheery song in the cold and lonely night, and how he had held our lives in his careful hands. And as I thought of this the helmsman ceased to sing, and I looked up and saw a pale light had appeared in the sky, and the lonely night had passed; and the dawn widened, and the sailors awoke.

And soon we saw the tide of the Sea himself advancing resolute between Yann's borders, and Yann sprang lithely at him and they struggled awhile; then Yann and all that was his were pushed back northward, so that the sailors had to hoist the sails and, the wind being favorable, we still held onwards.

And we passed Gondara and Narl and Haz. And we saw memorable, holy Golnuz, and heard the pilgrims praying.

When we awoke after the midday rest we were coming near to Nen, the last of the cities on the River Yann. And the jungle was all about us once again, and about Nen; but the great Mloon ranges stood up over all things, and watched the city from beyond the jungle.

Here we anchored, and the captain and I went up into the city and found that the Wanderers had come into Nen.

And the Wanderers were a weird, dark, tribe, that once in every seven years came down from the peaks of Mloon, having crossed by a pass that is known to them from some fantastic land that lies beyond. And the people of Nen were all outside their houses, and all stood wondering at their own streets. For the men and women of the Wanderers had crowded all the ways, and every one was doing some strange thing. Some danced astounding dances that they had learned from the desert wind, rapidly curving and swirling till the eye could follow no longer. Others played upon instruments beautiful wailing tunes that were full of horror, which souls had taught them lost by night in the desert, that strange far desert from which the Wanderers came.

None of their instruments were such as were known in Nen nor in any part of the region of the Yann; even the horns out of which some were made were of beasts that none had seen along the river, for they were barbed at the tips. And they sang, in the language of none, songs that seemed to be akin to the mysteries of night and to the unreasoned fear that haunts dark places.

Bitterly all the dogs of Nen distrusted them. And the Wanderers told one another fearful tales, for though no one in Nen knew ought of their language yet they could see the fear on the listeners' faces, and as the tale wound on the whites of their eyes showed vividly in terror as the eyes of some little beast whom the hawk has seized. Then the teller of the tale would smile and stop, and another would tell his story, and the teller of the first tale's lips would chatter with fear. And if some deadly snake chanced to appear the Wanderers would greet him as a brother, and the snake would seem to give his greetings to them before he passed on again. Once that most fierce and lethal of tropic snakes, the giant lythra, came out of the jungle and all down the street, the central street of Nen, and none of the Wanderers moved away from him, but they all played sonorously on drums, as though he had been a person of much honour; and the snake moved through the midst of them and smote none.

Even the Wanderers' children could do strange things, for if any one of them met with a child of Nen the two would stare at each other in silence with large grave eyes; then the Wanderers' child would slowly draw from his turban a live fish or snake. And the children of Nen could do nothing of that kind at all.

Much I should have wished to stay and hear the hymn with which they greet the night, that is answered by the wolves on the heights of Mloon, but it was now time to raise the anchor again that the captain might return from Bar-Wul-Yann upon the landward tide. So we went on board and continued down the Yann. And the captain and I spoke little, for we were thinking of our parting, which should be for long, and we watched instead the splendour of the westerning sun. For the sun was a ruddy gold, but a faint mist cloaked the jungle, lying low, and into it poured the smoke of the little jungle cities, and the smoke of them met together in the mist and joined into one haze, which became purple, and was lit by the sun, as the thoughts of men become hallowed by some great and sacred thing. Some times one column from a lonely house would rise up higher than the cities' smoke, and gleam by itself in the sun.

And now as the sun's last rays were nearly level, we saw the sight that I had come to see, for from two mountains that stood on either shore two cliffs of pink marble came out into the river, all glowing in the light of the low sun, and they were quite smooth and of mountainous altitude, and they nearly met, and Yann went tumbling between them and found the sea.

And this was Bar-Wul-Yann, the Gate of Yann, and in the distance through that barrier's gap I saw the azure indescribable sea, where little fishing-boats went gleaming by.

And the sun set, and the brief twilight came, and the exultation of the glory of Bar-Wul-Yann was gone, yet still the pink cliffs glowed, the fairest marvel that the eye beheld — and this in a land of wonders. And soon the twilight gave place to the coming out of stars, and the colours of Bar-Wul-Yann went dwindling away. And the sight of those cliffs was to me as some chord of music that a master's hand had launched from the violin, and which carries to Heaven or Faery the tremulous spirits of men.

And now by the shore they anchored and went no further, for they were sailors of the river and not of the sea, and knew the Yann but not the tides beyond.

And the time was come when the captain and I must part, he to go back to his fair Belzoond in sight of the distant peaks of the Hian Min, and I to find my way by strange means back to those hazy fields that all poets know, wherein stand small mysterious cottages through whose windows, looking westwards, you may see the fields of men, and looking eastwards see glittering elfin mountains, tipped with snow, going range on range into the region of Myth, and beyond it into the kingdom of Fantasy, which pertain to the Lands of Dream. Long we regarded one another, knowing that we should meet no more, for my fancy is weakening as the years slip by, and I go ever more seldom into the Lands of Dream. Then we clasped hands, uncouthly on his part, for it is not the method of greeting in his country, and he commended my soul to the care of his own gods, to his little lesser gods, the humble ones, to the gods that bless Belzoond.

A Tale of the Equator

He who is Sultan so remote to the East that his dominions were deemed fabulous in Babylon, whose name is a by-word for distance to-day in the streets of Bagdad, whose capital bearded travellers invoke by name in the gate at evening to gather hearers to their tales when the smoke of tobacco arises, dice rattle and taverns shine; even he in that very city made mandate, and said: "Let there be brought hither all my learned men that they may come before me and rejoice my heart with learning."

Men ran and clarions sounded, and it was so that there came before the Sultan all of his learned men. And many were found wanting. But of those that were able to say acceptable things, ever after to be named The Fortunate, one said that to the South of the Earth lay a Land — said Land was crowned with lotus — where it was summer in our winter days and where it was winter in summer.

And when the Sultan of those most distant lands knew that the Creator of All had contrived a device so vastly to his delight his merriment knew no bounds. On a sudden he spake and said, and this was the gist of his saying, that upon that line of boundary or limit that divided the North from the South a palace be made, where in the Northern courts should summer be, while in the south was winter; so should he move from court to court according to his mood, and dally with the summer in the morning and spend the noon with the snow. So the Sultan's poets were sent for and bade to tell of that city, foreseeing its splendour far away to the South and in the future of time; and some were found fortunate. And of those that were found fortunate and were crowned with flowers none earned more easily the Sultan's smile (on which long days depended) than he that foreseeing the city spake of it thus:

"In seven years and seven days, O Prop of Heaven, shall thy builders build it, thy palace that is neither North nor South, where neither winter nor summer is sole lord of the hours. White I see it, very vast, as a city, very fair, as a woman, Earth's wonder, with many windows, with thy princesses peering out at twilight; yea, I behold the bliss of the gold balconies, and hear a rustling down long galleries and the doves' coo upon its sculptured eaves. O Prop of Heaven, would that so fair a city were built by thine ancient sires, the children of the sun, that so might all men see it even to-day, and not the poets only, whose vision sees it so far away to the South and in the future of time.

"O King of the Years, it shall stand midmost on that line that divideth equally the North from the South and that parteth the seasons asunder as with a screen. On the Northern side when summer is in the North thy silken guards shall pace by dazzling walls while thy spearmen clad in furs go round the South. But at the hour of noon in the midmost day of the year thy chamberlain shall go down from his high place and into the midmost court, and men with trumpets shall go down behind him, and he shall utter a great cry at noon, and the men with trumpets shall cause their trumpets to blare, and the spearsmen clad in furs shall march round to the North and thy silken guard shall take their place in the South, and all the swallows shall rise and follow after. And alone in thine inner courts shall no change be, for they shall lie narrowly along that line that parteth the seasons in sunder and divideth the North from the South, and thy long gardens shall lie under them.

"And in thy gardens shall spring always be, for spring lies ever at the marge of summer; and autumn also shall always tint thy gardens, for autumn always flares at winter's edge, and those gardens shall lie apart between winter and summer. And there shall be orchards in thy garden, too, with all the burden of autumn on their boughs and all the blossom of spring.

"Yea, I behold this palace, for we see future things; I see its white wall shine in the huge glare of midsummer, and the lizards lying along it motionless in the sun, and men asleep in the noonday, and the butterflies floating by, and birds of radiant plumage chasing marvellous moths; far off the forest and great orchids glorying there, and iridescent insects dancing round in the light. I see the wall upon the other side; the snow has come upon the battlements, the icicles have fringed them like frozen beards, a wild wind blowing out of lonely places and crying to the cold fields as it blows has sent the snowdrifts higher than the buttresses; they that look out through windows on that side of thy palace see the wild geese flying low and all the birds of the winter, going by swift in packs beat low by the bitter wind, and the clouds above them are black, for it is midwinter there; while in thine other courts the fountains tinkle, falling on marble warmed by the fire of the summer sun.

"Such, O King of the Years, shall thy palace be, and its name shall be Erlathdronion, Earth's Wonder; and thy wisdom shall bid thine architects build at once, that all may see what as yet the poets see only, and that prophecy may be fulfilled."

And when the poet ceased the Sultan spake, and said, as all men hearkened with bent heads:

"It will be unnecessary for my builders to build this palace, Erlathdronion, Earth's Wonder, for in hearing thee we have drunk already its pleasures."

And the poet went forth from the Presence and dreamed a new thing.

Spring in Town

At a street corner sat, and played with a wind, Winter disconsolate.

Still tingled the fingers of the passers-by and still their breath was visible, and still they huddled their chins into their coats when turning a corner they met with a new wind, still windows lighted sent out into the street the thought of romantic comfort by evening fires; these things still were, yet the throne of Winter tottered, and every breeze brought tidings of further fortresses lost on lakes or boreal hill-slopes. And not any longer as a king did Winter appear in those streets, as when the city was decked with gleaming white to greet him as a conqueror and he rode in with his glittering icicles and haughty retinue of prancing winds, but he sat there with a little wind at the corner of the street like some old blind beggar with his hungry dog. And as to some old blind beggar Death approaches, and the alert ears of the sightless man prophetically hear his far-off footfall, so there came suddenly to Winter's ears the sound, from some neighbouring garden, of Spring approaching as she walked on daisies. And Spring approaching looked at huddled inglorious Winter.

"Begone," said Spring.

"There is nothing for you to do here," said Winter to her. Nevertheless he drew about him his grey and battered cloak and rose and called to his little bitter wind and up a side street that led northward strode away.

Pieces of paper and tall clouds of dust went with him as far as the city's outer gate. He turned then and called to Spring: "You can do nothing in this city," he said; then he marched homeward over plains and sea and heard his old winds howling as he marched. The ice broke up behind him and foundered like navies. To left and to right of him flew the flocks of the sea-birds, and far before him the geese's triumphant cry went like a clarion. Greater and greater grew his stature as he went northwards and ever more kingly his mien. Now he took baronies at a stride and now counties and came again to the snow-white frozen lands where the wolves came out to meet him and, draping himself anew with old grey clouds, strode through the gates of his invincible home, two old ice barriers swinging on pillars of ice that had never known the sun.

So the town was left to Spring. And she peered about to see what she could do with it. Presently she saw a dejected dog coming prowling down the road, so she sang to him and he gamboled. I saw him next day strutting with something of an air. Where there were trees she went to them and whispered, and they sang the arboreal song that only trees can hear, and the green buds came peeping out as stars while yet it is twilight, secretly one by one. She went to gardens and awaked from dreaming the warm maternal earth. In little patches bare and desolate she called up like a flame the golden crocus, or its purple brother like an emperor's ghost. She gladdened the graceless backs of untidy houses, here with a weed, there with a little grass. She said to the air, "Be joyous."

Children began to know that daisies blew in unfrequented corners. Buttonholes began to appear in the coats of the young men. The work of Spring was accomplished.

In the Twilight

The lock was quite crowded with boats when we capsized. I went down backwards for some few feet before I started to swim, then I came spluttering upwards towards the light; but, instead of reaching the surface, I hit my head against the keel of a boat and went down again. I struck out almost at once and came up, but before I reached the surface my head crashed against a boat for the second time, and I went right to the bottom. I was confused and thoroughly frightened. I was desperately in need of air, and knew that if I hit a boat for the third time I should never see the surface again. Drowning is a horrible death, notwithstanding all that has been said to the contrary. My past life never occurred to my mind, but I thought of many trivial things that I might not do or see again if I were drowned. I swam up in a slanting direction, hoping to avoid the boat that I had struck. Suddenly I saw all the boats in the lock quite clearly just above me, and every one of their curved varnished planks and the scratches and chips upon their keels. I saw several gaps among the boats where I might have swam up to the surface, but it did not seem worth while to try and get there, and I had forgotten why I wanted to. Then all the people leaned over the sides of their boats: I saw the light flannel suits of the men and the coloured flowers of the women's hats, and I noticed details of their dresses quite distinctly.

Everybody in the boats was looking down at me; then they all said to one another, "We must leave him now," and they and the boats went away; and there was nothing above me but the river and the sky, and on either side of me were the green weeds that grew in the mud, for I had somehow sunk back to the bottom again. The river as it flowed by murmured not unpleasantly in my ears, and the rushes seemed to be whispering quite softly among themselves. Presently the murmuring of the river took the form of words, and I heard it say, "We must go on to the sea; we must leave him now."

Then the river went away, and both its banks; and the rushes whispered, "Yes, we must leave him now." And they too departed, and I was left in a great emptiness staring up at the blue sky. Then the great sky bent over me, and spoke quite softly like a kindly nurse soothing some little foolish child, and the sky said, "Goodbye. All will be well. Goodbye." And I was sorry to lose the blue sky, but the sky went away. Then I was alone, with nothing round about me; I could see no light, but it was not dark — there was just absolutely nothing, above me and below me and on every side. I thought that perhaps I was dead, and that this might be eternity; when suddenly some great southern hills rose up all round about me, and I was lying on the warm, grassy slope of a valley in England. It was a valley that I had known well when I was young, but I had not seen it now for many years. Beside me stood the tall flower of the mint; I saw the sweet-smelling thyme flower and one or two wild strawberries. There came up to me from fields below me the beautiful smell of hay, and there was a break in the voice of the cuckoo. There was a feeling of summer and of evening and of lateness and of Sabbath in the air; the sky was calm and full of a strange colour, and the sun was low; the bells in the church in the village were all a-ring, and the chimes went wandering with echoes up the valley towards the sun, and whenever the echoes died a new chime was born. And all the people of the village walked up a stone-paved path under a black oak porch and went into the church, and the chimes stopped and the people of the village began to sing, and the level sunlight shone on the white tombstones that stood all round the church. Then there was a stillness in the village, and shouts and laughter came up from the valley no more, only the occasional sound of the organ and of song. And the blue butterflies, those that love the chalk, came and perched themselves on the tall grasses, five or six sometimes on a single piece of grass, and they closed their wings and slept, and the grass bent a little beneath them. And from the woods along the tops of the hills the rabbits came hopping out and nibbled the grass, and hopped a little further and nibbled again, and the large daisies closed their petals up and the birds began to sing.

Then the hills spoke, all the great chalk hills that I loved, and with a deep and solemn voice they said, "We have come to you to say Goodbye."

Then they all went away, and there was nothing again all round about me upon every side. I looked everywhere for something on which to rest the eye. Nothing. Suddenly a low grey sky swept over me and a moist air met my face; a great plain rushed up to me from the edge of the clouds; on two sides it touched the sky, and on two sides between it and the clouds a line of low hills lay. One line of hills brooded grey in the distance, the other stood a patchwork of little square green fields, with a few white cottages about it. The plain was an archipelago of a million islands each about a yard square or less, and every one of them was red with heather. I was back on the Bog of Allen again after many years, and it was just the same as ever, though I had heard that they were draining it. I was with an old friend whom I was glad to see again, for they had told me that he died some years ago. He seemed strangely young, but what surprised me most was that he stood upon a piece of bright green moss which I had always learned to think would never bear. I was glad, too, to see the old bog again and all the lovely things that grew there — the scarlet mosses and the green mosses and the firm and friendly heather, and the deep silent water. I saw a little stream that wandered vaguely through the bog, and little white shells down in the clear depths of it; I saw, a little way off, one of the great pools where no islands are, with rushes round its borders, where the ducks love to come. I looked long at that untroubled world of heather, and then I looked at the white cottages on the hill, and saw the grey smoke curling from their chimneys and knew that they burned turf there, and longed for the smell of burning turf again. And far away there arose and came nearer the weird cry of wild and happy voices, and a flock of geese appeared that was coming from the northward. Then their cries blended into one great voice of exultation, the voice of freedom, the voice of Ireland, the voice of the Waste; and the voice said "Goodbye to you. Goodbye!" and passed away into the distance; and as it passed, the tame geese on the farms cried out to their brothers up above them that they were free. Then the hills went away, and the bog and the sky went with them, and I was alone again, as lost souls are alone.

Then there grew up beside me the red brick buildings of my first school and the chapel that adjoined it. The fields a little way off were full of boys in white flannels playing cricket. On the asphalt playing ground, just by the schoolroom windows, stood Agamemnon, Achilles, and Odysseus, with their Argives behind them; but Hector stepped down out of a ground-floor window, and in the schoolroom were all Priam's sons and the Achaeans and fair Helen; and a little farther away the Ten Thousand drifted across the playground, going up into the heart of Persia to place Cyrus on his brother's throne. And the boys that I knew called to me from the fields, and said "Goodbye," and they and the fields went away; and the Ten Thousand said "Goodbye," each file as they passed me marching swiftly, and they too disappeared. And Hector and Agamemnon said "Goodbye," and the host of the Argives and the Achaeans; and they all went away and the old school with them, and I was alone again.

The next scene that filled the emptiness was rather dim: I was being led by my nurse along a little footpath over a common in Surrey. She was quite young. Close by a band of gypsies had lit their fire, near them their romantic caravan stood unhorsed, and the horse cropped grass beside it. It was evening, and the gypsies muttered round their fires in a tongue unknown and strange. Then they all said in English, "Goodbye." And the evening and the common and the camp-fire went away. And instead of this a white highway with darkness and stars below it that led into darkness and stars, but at the near end of the road were common fields and gardens, and there I stood close to a large number of people, men and women. And I saw a man walking alone down the road away from me towards the darkness and the stars, and all the people called him by his name, and the man would not hear them, but walked on down the road, and the people went on calling him by his name. But I became irritated with the man because he would not stop or turn round when so many people called him by his name, and it was a very strange name. And I became weary of hearing the strange name so very often repeated, so that I made a great effort to call him, that he might listen and that the people might stop repeating this strange name. And with the effort I opened my eyes wide, and the name that the people called was my own name, and I lay on the river's bank with men and women bending over me, and my hair was wet.

Wind and Fog

"Way for us," said the North Wind as he came down the sea on an errand of old Winter.

And he saw before him the grey silent fog that lay along the tides.

"Way for us," said the North Wind, "O ineffectual fog, for I am Winter's leader in his age-old war with the ships. I overwhelm them suddenly in my strength, or drive upon them the huge seafaring bergs. I cross an ocean while you move a mile. There is mourning in inland places when I have met the ships. I drive them upon the rocks and feed the sea. Wherever I appear they bow to our Lord the Winter."

And to his arrogant boasting nothing said the fog. Only he rose up slowly and trailed away from the sea and, crawling up long valleys, took refuge among the hills; and night came down and everything was still, and the fog began to mumble in the stillness. And I heard him telling infamously to himself the take of his horrible spoils. "A hundred and fifteen galleons of old Spain, a certain argosy that went from Tyre, eight fisher-fleets and ninety ships of the line, twelve warships under sail, with their cannonades, three hundred and eighty-seven river-craft, forty-two merchantmen that carried spice, thirty yachts, twenty-one battleships of the modern time, nine thousand admirals.....” he mumbled and chuckled on, till I suddenly rose and fled from his fearful contamination.

A Story of Land and Sea

It is written in the first Book of Wonder how Captain Shard of the bad ship Desperate Lark, having looted the seacoast city Bombasharna, retired from active life; and resigning piracy to younger men, with the good will of the North and South Atlantic, settled down with a captured queen on his floating island.

Sometimes he sank a ship for the sake of old times but he no longer hovered along the trade-routes; and timid merchants watched for other men.

It was not age that caused him to leave his romantic profession; nor unworthiness of its traditions, nor gun-shot wound, nor drink; but grim necessity and force majeure. Five navies were after him. How he gave them the slip one day in the Mediterranean, how he fought with the Arabs, how a ship's broadside was heard in Lat. 23 N. Long. 4 E. for the first time and the last, with other things unknown to Admiralties, I shall proceed to tell.

He had had his fling, had Shard, captain of pirates, and all his merry men wore pearls in their ear-rings; and now the English fleet was after him under full sail along the coast of Spain with a good North wind behind them. They were not gaining much on Shard's rakish craft, the bad ship Desperate Lark, yet they were closer than was to his liking, and they interfered with business.

For a day and a night they had chased him, when off Cape St. Vincent at about six a. m. Shard took that step that decided his retirement from active life, he turned for the Mediterranean. Had he held on Southwards down the African coast it is doubtful whether in face of the interference of England, Russia, France, Denmark and Spain, he could have made piracy pay; but in turning for the Mediterranean, he took what we may call the penultimate step of his life which meant for him settling down. There were three great courses of action invented by Shard in his youth, upon which he pondered by day and brooded by night, consolations in all his dangers, secret even from his men, three means of escape as he hoped from any peril that might meet him on the sea. One of these was the floating island that the Book of Wonder tells of, another was so fantastic that we may doubt if even the brilliant audacity of Shard could ever have found it practicable, at least he never tried it so far as is known in that tavern by the sea in which I glean my news, and the third he determined on carrying out as he turned that morning for the Mediterranean. True he might yet have practised piracy in spite of the step that he took, a little later when the seas grew quiet, but that penultimate step was like that small house in the country that the business man has his eye on, like some snug investment put away for old age, there are certain final courses in men's lives which after taking they never go back to business.

He turned then for the Mediterranean with the English fleet behind him, and his men wondered.

What madness was this, — muttered Bill the Boatswain in Old Frank's only ear, — with the French fleet waiting in the Gulf of Lyons and the Spaniards all the way between Sardinia and Tunis: for they knew the Spaniards' ways. And they made a deputation and waited upon Captain Shard, all of them sober and wearing their costly clothes, and they said that the Mediterranean was a trap, and all he said was that the North wind should hold. And the crew said they were done.

So they entered the Mediterranean and the English fleet came up and closed the straits. And Shard went tacking along the Moroccan coast with a dozen frigates behind him. And the North wind grew in strength. And not till evening did he speak to his crew, and then he gathered them all together except the man at the helm, and politely asked them to come down to the hold. And there he showed them six immense steel axles and a dozen low iron wheels of enormous width which none had seen before; and he told his crew how all unknown to the world his keel had been specially fitted for these same axles and wheels, and how he meant soon to sail the wide Atlantic again, though not by way of the straits. And when they heard the name of the Atlantic all his merry men cheered, for they looked on the Atlantic as a wide safe sea.

And night came down and Captain Shard sent for his diver. With the sea getting up it was hard work for the diver, but by midnight things were done to Shard's satisfaction, and the diver said that of all the jobs he had done — but finding no apt comparison, and being in need of a drink, silence fell on him and soon sleep, and his comrades carried him away to his hammock. All the next day the chase went on with the English well in sight, for Shard had lost time overnight with his wheels and axles, and the danger of meeting the Spaniards increased every hour; and evening came when every minute seemed dangerous, yet they still went tacking on towards the East where they knew the Spaniards must be.

And at last they sighted their topsails right ahead, and still Shard went on. It was a close thing, but night was coming on, and the Union Jack which he hoisted helped Shard with the Spaniards for the last few anxious minutes, though it seemed to anger the English, but as Shard said, "There's no pleasing everyone," and then the twilight shivered into darkness.

"Hard to starboard," said Captain Shard.

The North wind which had risen all day was now blowing a gale. I do not know what part of the coast Shard steered for, but Shard knew, for the coasts of the world were to him what Margate is to some of us.

At a place where the desert rolling up from mystery and from death, yea, from the heart of Africa, emerges upon the sea, no less grand than her, no less terrible, even there they sighted the land quite close, almost in darkness. Shard ordered every man to the hinder part of the ship and all the ballast too; and soon the Desperate Lark, her prow a little high out of the water, doing her eighteen knots before the wind, struck a sandy beach and shuddered, she heeled over a little, then righted herself, and slowly headed into the interior of Africa.

The men would have given three cheers, but after the first Shard silenced them and, steering the ship himself, he made them a short speech while the broad wheels pounded slowly over the African sand, doing barely five knots in a gale. The perils of the sea he said had been greatly exaggerated. Ships had been sailing the sea for hundreds of years and at sea you knew what to do, but on land this was different. They were on land now and they were not to forget it. At sea you might make as much noise as you pleased and no harm was done, but on land anything might happen. One of the perils of the land that he instanced was that of hanging. For every hundred men that they hung on land, he said, not more than twenty would be hung at sea. The men were to sleep at their guns. They would not go far that night; for the risk of being wrecked at night was another danger peculiar to the land, while at sea you might sail from set of sun till dawn: yet it was essential to get out of sight of the sea for if anyone knew they were there they'd have cavalry after them. And he had sent back Smerdrak (a young lieutenant of pirates) to cover their tracks where they came up from the sea. And the merry men vigorously nodded their heads though they did not dare to cheer, and presently Smerdrak came running up and they threw him a rope by the stern. And when they had done fifteen knots they anchored, and Captain Shard gathered his men about him and, standing by the land-wheel in the bows, under the large and clear Algerian stars, he explained his system of steering. There was not much to be said for it, he had with considerable ingenuity detached and pivoted the portion of the keel that held the leading axle and could move it by chains which were controlled from the land-wheel, thus the front pair of wheels could be deflected at will, but only very slightly, and they afterwards found that in a hundred yards they could only turn their ship four yards from her course. But let not captains of comfortable battleships, or owners even of yachts, criticise too harshly a man who was not of their time and who knew not modern contrivances; it should be remembered also that Shard was no longer at sea. His steering may have been clumsy but he did what he could.

When the use and limitations of his land-wheel had been made clear to his men, Shard bade them all turn in except those on watch. Long before dawn he woke them and by the very first gleam of light they got their ship under way, so that when those two fleets that had made so sure of Shard closed in like a great crescent on the Algerian coast there was no sign to see of the Desperate Lark either on sea or land; and the flags of the Admiral's ship broke out into a hearty English oath.

The gale blew for three days and, Shard using more sail by daylight, they scudded over the sands at little less than ten knots, though on the report of rough water ahead (as the lookout man called rocks, low hills or uneven surfaces before he adapted himself to his new surroundings) the rate was much decreased. Those were long summer days and Shard who was anxious while the wind held good to outpace the rumour of his own appearance sailed for nineteen hours a day, lying to at ten in the evening and hoisting sail again at three a. m. when it first began to be light.

In those three days he did five hundred miles; then the wind dropped to a breeze though it still blew from the North, and for a week they did no more than two knots an hour. The merry men began to murmur then. Luck had distinctly favoured Shard at first for it sent him at ten knots through the only populous districts well ahead of crowds except those who chose to run, and the cavalry were away on a local raid. As for the runners they soon dropped off when Shard pointed his cannon though he did not dare to fire, up there near the coast; for much as he jeered at the intelligence of the English and Spanish Admirals in not suspecting his manoeuvre, the only one as he said that was possible in the circumstances, yet he knew that cannon had an obvious sound which would give his secret away to the weakest mind. Certainly luck had befriended him, and when it did so no longer he made out of the occasion all that could be made; for instance while the wind held good he had never missed opportunities to revictual, if he passed by a village its pigs and poultry were his, and whenever he passed by water he filled his tanks to the brim, and now that he could only do two knots he sailed all night with a man and a lantern before him; thus in that week he did close on four hundred miles while another man would have anchored at night and have missed five or six hours out of the twenty-four. Yet his men murmured. Did he think the wind would last for ever, they said. And Shard only smoked. It was clear that he was thinking, and thinking hard. "But what is he thinking about?" said Bill to Bad Jack. And Bad Jack answered: "He may think as hard as he likes but thinking won't get us out of the Sahara if this wind were to drop."

And towards the end of that week Shard went to his chart-room and laid a new course for his ship a little to the East and towards cultivation. And one day towards evening they sighted a village, and twilight came and the wind dropped altogether. Then the murmurs of the merry men grew to oaths and nearly to mutiny. "Where were they now?" they asked, "and were they being treated like poor honest men?"

Shard quieted them by asking what they wished to do themselves and when no one had any better plan than going to the villagers and saying that they had been blown out of their course by a storm, Shard unfolded his scheme to them.

Long ago he had heard how they drove carts with oxen in Africa, oxen were very numerous in these parts wherever there was any cultivation, and for this reason when the wind had begun to drop he had laid his course for the village: that night the moment it was dark they were to drive off fifty yoke of oxen; by midnight they must all be yoked to the bows and then away they would go at a good round gallop.

So fine a plan as this astonished the men and they all apologised for their want of faith in Shard, shaking hands with him every one and spitting on their hands before they did so in token of good will.

The raid that night succeeded admirably, but ingenious as Shard was on land, and a past-master at sea, yet it must be admitted that lack of experience in this class of seamanship led him to make a mistake, a slight one it is true, and one that a little practice would have prevented altogether: the oxen could not gallop. Shard swore at them, threatened them with his pistol, said they should have no food, and all to no avail: that night and as long as they pulled the bad ship Desperate Lark they did one knot an hour and no more. Shard's failures like everything that came his way were used as stones in the edifice of his future success, he went at once to his chart-room and worked out all his calculations anew.

The matter of the oxen's pace made pursuit impossible to avoid. Shard therefore countermanded his order to his lieutenant to cover the tracks in the sand, and the Desperate Lark plodded on into the Sahara on her new course trusting to her guns.

The village was not a large one and the little crowd that was sighted astern next morning disappeared after the first shot from the cannon in the stern. At first Shard made the oxen wear rough iron bits, another of his mistakes, and strong bits too. "For if they run away," he had said, "we might as well be driving before a gale and there's no saying where we'd find ourselves," but after a day or two he found that the bits were no good and, like the practical man he was, immediately corrected his mistake.

And now the crew sang merry songs all day bringing out mandolins and clarionets and cheering Captain Shard. All were jolly except the captain himself whose face was moody and perplexed; he alone expected to hear more of those villagers; and the oxen were drinking up the water every day, he alone feared that there was no more to be had, and a very unpleasant fear that is when your ship is becalmed in a desert. For over a week they went on like this doing ten knots a day and the music and singing got on the captain's nerves, but he dared not tell his men what the trouble was. And then one day the oxen drank up the last of the water. And Lieutenant Smerdrak came and reported the fact.

"Give them rum," said Shard, and he cursed the oxen.

"What is good enough for me," he said, "should be good enough for them," and he swore that they should have rum.

"Aye, aye, sir," said the young lieutenant of pirates. Shard should not be judged by the orders he gave that day, for nearly a fortnight he had watched the doom that was coming slowly towards him, discipline cut him off from anyone that might have shared his fear and discussed it, and all the while he had had to navigate his ship, which even at sea is an arduous responsibility. These things had fretted the calm of that clear judgement that had once baffled five navies. Therefore he cursed the oxen and ordered them rum, and Smerdrak had said "Aye, aye, sir," and gone below.

Towards sunset Shard was standing on the poop, thinking of death; it would not come to him by thirst; mutiny first, he thought. The oxen were refusing rum for the last time, and the men were beginning to eye Captain Shard in a very ominous way, not muttering, but each man looking at him with a sidelong look of the eye as though there were only one thought among them all that had no need of words. A score of geese like a long letter "V" were crossing the evening sky, they slanted their necks and all went twisting downwards somewhere about the horizon. Captain Shard rushed to his chart-room, and presently the men came in at the door with Old Frank in front looking awkward and twisting his cap in his hand.

"What is it?" said Shard as though nothing were wrong. Then Old Frank said what he had come to say: "We want to know what you be going to do."

And the men nodded grimly.

"Get water for the oxen," said Captain Shard, "as the swine won't have rum, and they'll have to work for it, the lazy beasts. Up anchor!"

And at the word water a look came into their faces like when some wanderer suddenly thinks of home.

"Water!" they said.

"Why not?" said Captain Shard. And none of them ever knew that but for those geese, that slanted their necks and suddenly twisted downwards, they would have found no water that night nor ever after, and the Sahara would have taken them as she has taken so many and shall take so many more. All that night they followed their new course: at dawn they found an oasis and the oxen drank.

And here, on this green acre or so with its palm-trees and its well, beleaguered by thousands of miles of desert and holding out through the ages, here they decided to stay: for those who have been without water for a while in one of Africa's deserts come to have for that simple fluid such a regard as you, O reader, might not easily credit. And here each man chose a site where he would build his hut, and settle down, and marry perhaps, and even forget the sea; when Captain Shard having filled his tanks and barrels peremptorily ordered them to weigh anchor.

There was much dissatisfaction, even some grumbling, but when a man has twice saved his fellows from death by the sheer freshness of his mind they come to have a respect for his judgement that is not shaken by trifles. It must be remembered that in the affair of the dropping of the wind and again when they ran out of water those men were at their wits' end: so was Shard on the last occasion, but that they did not know. All this Shard knew, and he chose this occasion to strengthen the reputation that he had in the minds of the men of that bad ship by explaining to them his motives, which usually he kept secret. The oasis he said must be a port of call for all the travellers within hundreds of miles: how many men did you see gathered together in any part of the world where there was a drop of whiskey to be had! And water here was much rarer than whiskey in decent countries and, such was the peculiarity of the Arabs, even more precious. Another thing he pointed out to them, the Arabs were a singularly inquisitive people and if they came upon a ship in the desert they would probably talk about it; and the world having a wickedly malicious tongue would never construe in its proper light their difference with the English and Spanish fleets, but would merely side with the strong against the weak.

And the men sighed, and sang the capstan song and hoisted the anchor and yoked the oxen up, and away they went doing their steady knot, which nothing could increase. It may be thought strange that with all sail furled in dead calm and while the oxen rested they should have cast anchor at all. But custom is not easily overcome and long survives its use. Rather enquire how many such useless customs we ourselves preserve: the flaps for instance to pull up the tops of hunting-boots though the tops no longer pull up, the bows on our evening shoes that neither tie nor untie. They said they felt safer that way and there was an end of it.

Shard lay a course of South by West and they did ten knots that day, the next day they did seven or eight and Shard hove to. Here he intended to stop, they had huge supplies of fodder on board for the oxen, for his men he had a pig or so, plenty of poultry, several sacks of biscuits and ninety-eight oxen (for two were already eaten), and they were only twenty miles from water. Here he said they would stay till folks forgot their past, someone would invent something or some new thing would turn up to take folks' minds off them and the ships he had sunk: he forgot that there are men who are well paid to remember.

Half way between him and the oasis he established a little depot where he buried his water-barrels. As soon as a barrel was empty he sent half a dozen men to roll it by turns to the depot. This they would do at night, keeping hid by day, and next night they would push it on to the oasis, fill the barrel and roll it back. Thus only ten miles away he soon had a store of water, unknown to the thirstiest native of Africa, from which he could safely replenish his tanks at will. He allowed his men to sing and even within reason to light fires. Those were jolly nights while the rum held out; sometimes they saw gazelles watching them curiously, sometimes a lion went by over the sand, the sound of his roar added to their sense of the security of their ship; all round them level, immense lay the Sahara: "This is better than an English prison," said Captain Shard.

And still the dead calm lasted, not even the sand whispered at night to little winds; and when the rum gave out and it looked like trouble, Shard reminded them what little use it had been to them when it was all they had and the oxen wouldn't look at it.

And the days wore on with singing, and even dancing at times, and at nights round a cautious fire in a hollow of sand with only one man on watch they told tales of the sea. It was all a relief after arduous watches and sleeping by the guns, a rest to strained nerves and eyes; and all agreed, for all that they missed their rum, that the best place for a ship like theirs was the land.

This was Latitude 23 North, Longitude 4 East, where, as I have said, a ship's broadside was heard for the first time and the last. It happened this way.

They had been there several weeks and had eaten perhaps ten or a dozen oxen and all that while there had been no breath of wind and they had seen no one: when one morning about two bells when the crew were at breakfast the lookout man reported cavalry on the port side. Shard who had already surrounded his ship with sharpened stakes ordered all his men on board, the young trumpeter who prided himself on having picked up the ways of the land, sounded "Prepare to receive cavalry"; Shard sent a few men below with pikes to the lower port-holes, two more aloft with muskets, the rest to the guns, he changed the "grape" or "canister" with which the guns were loaded in case of surprise, for shot, cleared the decks, drew in ladders, and before the cavalry came within range everything was ready for them. The oxen were always yoked in order that Shard could manoeuvre his ship at a moment's notice.

When first sighted the cavalry were trotting but they were coming on now at a slow canter, Arabs in white robes on good horses. Shard estimated that there were two or three hundred of them. At sixty yards Shard opened with one gun, he had had the distance measured, but had never practised for fear of being heard at the oasis: the shot went high. The next one fell short and ricochetted over the Arabs' heads. Shard had the range then and by the time the ten remaining guns of his broadside were given the same elevation as that of his second gun the Arabs had come to the spot where the last shot pitched. The broadside hit the horses, mostly low, and ricochetted amongst them; one cannon-ball striking a rock at the horses' feet shattered it and sent fragments flying amongst the Arabs with the peculiar scream of things set free by projectiles from their motionless harmless state, and the cannon-ball went on with them with a great howl, this shot alone killed three men.

"Very satisfactory," said Shard rubbing his chin. "Load with grape," he added sharply.

The broadside did not stop the Arabs nor even reduce their speed but they crowded in closer together as though for company in their time of danger, which they should not have done. They were four hundred yards off now, three hundred and fifty; and then the muskets began, for the two men in the crow's-nest had thirty loaded muskets besides a few pistols, the muskets all stood round them leaning against the rail; they picked them up and fired them one by one. Every shot told, but still the Arabs came on. They were galloping now. It took some time to load the guns in those days. Three hundred yards, two hundred and fifty, men dropping all the way, two hundred yards; Old Frank for all his one ear had terrible eyes; it was pistols now, they had fired all their muskets; a hundred and fifty; Shard had marked the fifties with little white stones. Old Frank and Bad Jack up aloft felt pretty uneasy when they saw the Arabs had come to that little white stone, they both missed their shots.

"All ready?" said Captain Shard.

"Aye, aye, sir," said Smerdrak.

"Right," said Captain Shard raising a finger.

A hundred and fifty yards is a bad range at which to be caught by grape (or "case" as we call it now), the gunners can hardly miss and the charge has time to spread. Shard estimated afterwards that he got thirty Arabs by that broadside alone and as many horses.

There were close on two hundred of them still on their horses, yet the broadside of grape had unsettled them, they surged round the ship but seemed doubtful what to do. They carried swords and scimitars in their hands, though most had strange long muskets slung behind them, a few unslung them and began firing wildly. They could not reach Shard's merry men with their swords. Had it not been for that broadside that took them when it did they might have climbed up from their horses and carried the bad ship by sheer force of numbers, but they would have had to have been very steady, and the broadside spoiled all that. Their best course was to have concentrated all their efforts in setting fire to the ship but this they did not attempt. Part of them swarmed all round the ship brandishing their swords and looking vainly for an easy entrance; perhaps they expected a door, they were not sea-faring people; but their leaders were evidently set on driving off the oxen not dreaming that the Desperate Lark had other means of travelling. And this to some extent they succeeded in doing. Thirty they drove off, cutting the traces, twenty they killed on the spot with their scimitars though the bow gun caught them twice as they did their work, and ten more were unluckily killed by Shard's bow gun. Before they could fire a third time from the bows they all galloped away, firing back at the oxen with their muskets and killing three more, and what troubled Shard more than the loss of his oxen was the way that they manoeuvred, galloping off just when the bow gun was ready and riding off by the port bow where the broadside could not get them, which seemed to him to show more knowledge of guns than they could have learned on that bright morning. What, thought Shard to himself, if they should bring big guns against the Desperate Lark! And the mere thought of it made him rail at Fate. But the merry men all cheered when they rode away. Shard had only twenty-two oxen left, and then a score or so of the Arabs dismounted while the rest rode further on leading their horses. And the dismounted men lay down on the port bow behind some rocks two hundred yards away and began to shoot at the oxen. Shard had just enough of them left to manoeuvre his ship with an effort and he turned his ship a few points to the starboard so as to get a broadside at the rocks. But grape was of no use here as the only way he could get an Arab was by hitting one of the rocks with shot behind which an Arab was lying, and the rocks were not easy to hit except by chance, and as often as he manoeuvred his ship the Arabs changed their ground. This went on all day while the mounted Arabs hovered out of range watching what Shard would do; and all the while the oxen were growing fewer, so good a mark were they, until only ten were left, and the ship could manoeuvre no longer. But then they all rode off.

The merry men were delighted, they calculated that one way and another they had unhorsed a hundred Arabs and on board there had been no more than one man wounded: Bad Jack had been hit in the wrist;

probably by a bullet meant for the men at the guns, for the Arabs were firing high. They had captured a horse and had found quaint weapons on the bodies of the dead Arabs and an interesting kind of tobacco. It was evening now and they talked over the fight, made jokes about their luckier shots, smoked their new tobacco and sang; altogether it was the jolliest evening they'd had. But Shard alone on the quarter-deck paced to and fro pondering, brooding and wondering. He had chopped off Bad Jack's wounded hand and given him a hook out of store, for captain does doctor upon these occasions and Shard, who was ready for most things, kept half a dozen or so neat new limbs, and of course a chopper. Bad Jack had gone below swearing a little and said he'd lie down for a bit, the men were smoking and singing on the sand, and Shard was there alone. The thought that troubled Shard was: What would the Arabs do? They did not look like men to go away for nothing. And at the back of all his thoughts was one that reiterated guns, guns, guns. He argued with himself that they could not drag them all that way on the sand, that the Desperate Lark was not worth it, that they had given it up. Yet he knew in his heart that that was what they would do. He knew there were fortified towns in Africa, and as for its being worth it, he knew that there was no pleasant thing left now to those defeated men except revenge, and if the Desperate Lark had come over the sand why not guns? He knew that the ship could never hold out against guns and cavalry, a week perhaps, two weeks, even three: what difference did it make how long it was, and the men sang:

Away we go,
Oho, Oho, Oho,
A drop of rum for you and me
And the world's as round as the letter O
And round it runs the sea.

A melancholy settled down on Shard.

About sunset Lieutenant Smerdrak came up for orders. Shard ordered a trench to be dug along the port side of the ship. The men wanted to sing and grumbled at having to dig, especially as Shard never mentioned his fear of guns, but he fingered his pistols and in the end Shard had his way. No one on board could shoot like Captain Shard. This is often the way with captains of pirate ships, it is a difficult position to hold. Discipline is essential to those that have the right to fly the skull-and-cross-bones, and Shard was the man to enforce it. It was starlight by the time the trench was dug to captain's satisfaction and the men that it was to protect when the worst came to the worst swore all the time as they dug. And when it was finished they clamoured to make a feast on some of the killed oxen, and this Shard let them do. And they lit a huge fire for the first time, burning abundant scrub, they thinking that Arabs daren't return, Shard knowing that concealment was now useless. All that night they feasted and sang, and Shard sat up in his chart-room making his plans.

When morning came they rigged up the cutter as they called the captured horse and told off her crew. As there were only two men that could ride at all these became the crew of the cutter. Spanish Dick and Bill the Boatswain were the two.

Shard's orders were that turn and turn about they should take command of the cutter and cruise about five miles off to the North East all the day but at night they were to come in. And they fitted the horse up with a flagstaff in front of the saddle so that they could signal from her, and carried an anchor behind for fear she should run away.

And as soon as Spanish Dick had ridden off Shard sent some men to roll all the barrels back from the depot where they were buried in the sand, with orders to watch the cutter all the time and, if she signalled, to return as fast as they could.

They buried the Arabs that day, removing their water-bottles and any provisions they had, and that night they got all the water-barrels in, and for days nothing happened. One event of extraordinary importance did indeed occur, the wind got up one day, but it was due South, and as the oasis lay to the North of them and beyond that they might pick up the camel track Shard decided to stay where he was. If it had looked to him like lasting Shard might have hoisted sail but it dropped at evening as he knew it would, and in any case it was not the wind he wanted. And more days went by, two weeks without a breeze. The dead oxen would not keep and they had had to kill three more, there were only seven left now.

Never before had the men been so long without rum. And Captain Shard had doubled the watch besides making two more men sleep at the guns. They had tired of their simple games, and most of their songs, and their tales that were never true were no longer new. And then one day the monotony of the desert came down upon them.

There is a fascination in the Sahara, a day there is delightful, a week is pleasant, a fortnight is a matter of opinion, but it was running into months. The men were perfectly polite but the boatswain wanted to know when Shard thought of moving on. It was an unreasonable question to ask of the captain of any ship in a dead calm in a desert, but Shard said he would set a course and let him know in a day or two. And a day or two went by over the monotony of the Sahara, who for monotony is unequalled by all the parts of the earth. Great marshes cannot equal it, nor plains of grass nor the sea, the Sahara alone lies unaltered by the seasons, she has no altering surface, no flowers to fade or grow, year in year out she is changeless for hundreds and hundreds of miles. And the boatswain came again and took off his cap and asked Captain Shard to be so kind as to tell them about his new course. Shard said he meant to stay until they had eaten three more of the oxen as they could only take three of them in the hold, there were only six left now. But what if there was no wind, the boatswain said. And at that moment the faintest breeze from the North ruffled the boatswain's forelock as he stood with his cap in his hand.

"Don't talk about the wind to *me*," said Captain Shard; and Bill was a little frightened for Shard's mother had been a gipsy.

But it was only a breeze astray, a trick of the Sahara.

And another week went by and they ate two more oxen.

They obeyed Captain Shard ostentatiously now but they wore ominous looks. Bill came again and Shard answered him in Romany.

Things were like this one hot Sahara morning when the cutter signalled. The lookout man told Shard and Shard read the message, "Cavalry astern" it read, and then a little later she signalled, "With guns."

"Ah," said Captain Shard.

One ray of hope Shard had; the flags on the cutter fluttered. For the first time for five weeks a light breeze blew from the North, very light, you hardly felt it. Spanish Dick rode in and anchored his horse to starboard and the cavalry came on slowly from the port.

Not till the afternoon did they come in sight, and all the while that little breeze was blowing.

"One knot," said Shard at noon. "Two knots," he said at six bells and still it grew and the Arabs trotted nearer. By five o'clock the merry men of the bad ship Desperate Lark could make out twelve long old-fashioned guns on low wheeled carts dragged by horses and what looked like lighter guns carried on camels. The wind was blowing a little stronger now. "Shall we hoist sail, sir?" said Bill.

"Not yet," said Shard.

By six o'clock the Arabs were just outside the range of cannon and there they halted. Then followed an anxious hour or so, but the Arabs came no nearer. They evidently meant to wait till dark to bring their guns up. Probably they intended to dig a gun epaulment from which they could safely pound away at the ship.

"We could do three knots," said Shard half to himself as he was walking up and down his quarter-deck with very fast short paces. And then the sun set and they heard the Arabs praying and Shard's merry men cursed at the top of their voices to show that they were as good men as they.

The Arabs had come no nearer, waiting for night. They did not know how Shard was longing for it too, he was gritting his teeth and sighing for it, he even would have prayed, but that he feared that it might remind Heaven of him and his merry men.

Night came and the stars. "Hoist sail," said Shard. The men sprang to their places, they had had enough of that silent lonely spot. They took the oxen on board and let the great sails down, and like a lover coming from over sea, long dreamed of, long expected, like a lost friend seen again after many years, the North wind came into the pirates' sails. And before Shard could stop it a ringing English cheer went away to the wondering Arabs.

They started off at three knots and soon they might have done four but Shard would not risk it at night. All night the wind held good, and doing three knots from ten to four they were far out of sight of the Arabs when daylight came. And then Shard hoisted more sail and they did four knots and by eight bells they were doing four and a half. The spirits of those volatile men rose high, and discipline became perfect. So long as there was wind in the sails and water in the tanks Captain Shard felt safe at least from mutiny. Great men can only be overthrown while their fortunes are at their lowest. Having failed to depose Shard when his plans were open to criticism and he himself scarce knew what to do next it was hardly likely they could do it now; and whatever we think of his past and his way of living we cannot deny that Shard was among the great men of the world.

Of defeat by the Arabs he did not feel so sure. It was useless to try to cover his tracks even if he had had time, the Arab cavalry could have picked them up anywhere. And he was afraid of their camels with those light guns on board, he had heard they could do seven knots and keep it up most of the day and if as much as one shot struck the mainmast... and Shard taking his mind off useless fears worked out on his chart when the Arabs were likely to overtake them. He told his men that the wind would hold good for a week, and, gipsy or no, he certainly knew as much about thc wind as is good for a sailor to know.

Alone in his chart-room he worked it out like this, mark two hours to the good for surprise and finding the tracks and delay in starting, say three hours if the guns were mounted in their epaulments, then the Arabs should start at seven. Supposing the camels go twelve hours a day at seven knots they would do eighty-four knots a day, while Shard doing three knots from ten to four, and four knots the rest of the time, was doing ninety and actually gaining. But when it came to it he wouldn't risk more than two knots at night while the enemy were out of sight, for he rightly regarded anything more than that as dangerous when sailing on land at night, so he too did eighty-four knots a day. It was a pretty race. I have not troubled to see if Shard added up his figures wrongly or if he underrated the pace of camels, but whatever it was the Arabs gained slightly, for on the fourth day Spanish Jack, five knots astern on what they called the cutter, sighted the camels a very long way off and signalled the fact to Shard. They had left their cavalry behind as Shard supposed they would. The wind held good, they still had two oxen left and could always eat their "cutter", and they had a fair, though not ample, supply of water, but the appearance of the Arabs was a blow to Shard for it showed him that there was no getting away from them, and of all things he dreaded guns. He made light of it to the men: said they would sink the lot before they had been in action half an hour: yet he feared that once the guns came up it was only a question of time before his rigging was cut or his steering gear disabled.

One point the Desperate Lark scored over the Arabs and a very good one too, darkness fell just before they could have sighted her and now Shard used the lantern ahead as he dared not do on the first night when the Arabs were close, and with the help of it managed to do three knots. The Arabs encamped in the evening and the Desperate Lark gained twenty knots. But the next evening they appeared again and this time they saw the sails of the Desperate Lark.

On the sixth day they were close. On the seventh they were closer. And then, a line of verdure across their bows, Shard saw the Niger River.

Whether he knew that for a thousand miles it rolled its course through forest, whether he even knew that it was there at all; what his plans were, or whether he lived from day to day like a man whose days are numbered he never told his men. Nor can I get an indication on this point from the talk that I hear from sailors in their cups in a certain tavern I know of. His face was expressionless, his mouth shut, and he held his ship to her course. That evening they were up to the edge of the tree trunks and the Arabs camped and waited ten knots astern and the wind had sunk a little.

There Shard anchored a little before sunset and landed at once. At first he explored the forest a little on foot. Then he sent for Spanish Dick. They had slung the cutter on board some days ago when they found she could not keep up. Shard could not ride but he sent for Spanish Dick and told him he must take him as a passenger. So Spanish Dick slung him in front of the saddle "before the mast" as Shard called it, for they still carried a mast on the front of the saddle, and away they galloped together. "Rough weather," said Shard, but he surveyed the forest as he went and the long and short of it was he found a place where the forest was less than half a mile thick and the Desperate Lark might get through: but twenty trees must be cut. Shard marked the trees himself, sent Spanish Dick right back to watch the Arabs, and turned the whole of his crew on to those twenty trees. It was a frightful risk, the Desperate Lark was empty, with an enemy no more than ten knots astern, but it was a moment for bold measures and Shard took the chance of being left without his ship in the heart of Africa in the hope of being repaid by escaping altogether.

The men worked all night on those twenty trees, those that had no axes bored with bradawls and blasted, and then relieved those that had.

Shard was indefatigable, he went from tree to tree showing exactly what way every one was to fall, and what was to be done with them when they were down. Some had to be cut down because their branches would get in the way of the masts, others because their trunks would be in the way of the wheels; in the case of the last the stumps had to be made smooth and low with saws and perhaps a bit of the trunk sawn off and rolled away. This was the hardest work they had. And they were all large trees, on the other hand had they been small there would have been many more of them and they could not have sailed in and out, sometimes for hundreds of yards, without cutting any at all: and all this Shard calculated on doing if only there was time.

The light before dawn came and it looked as if they would never do it at all. And then dawn came and it was all done but one tree, the hardest part of the work had all been done in the night and a sort of final rush cleared everything up except that one huge tree. And then the cutter signalled the Arabs were moving. At dawn they had prayed, and now they had struck their camp. Shard at once ordered all his men to the ship except ten whom he left at the tree, they had some way to go and the Arabs had been moving some ten minutes before they got there. Shard took in the cutter which wasted five minutes, hoisted sail short-handed and that took give minutes more, and slowly got under way.

The wind was dropping still and by the time the Desperate Lark had come to the edge of that part of the forest through which Shard had laid his course the Arabs were no more than five knots away. He had sailed East half a mile, which he ought to have done overnight so as to be ready, but he could not spare time or thought or men away from those twenty trees. Then Shard turned into the forest and the Arabs were dead astern. They hurried when they saw the Desperate Lark enter the forest.

"Doing ten knots," said Shard as he watched them from the deck. The Desperate Lark was doing no more than a knot and a half for the wind was weak under the lee of the trees. Yet all went well for a while. The big tree had just come down some way ahead, and the ten men were sawing bits off the trunk.

And then Shard saw a branch that he had not marked on the chart, it would just catch the top of the mainmast. He anchored at once and sent a hand aloft who sawed it half way through and did the rest with a pistol, and now the Arabs were only three knots astern. For a quarter of a mile Shard steered them through the forest till they came to the ten men and that big bad tree, another foot had yet to come off one corner of the stump for the wheels had to pass over it. Shard turned all hands on to the stump and it was then that the Arabs came within shot. But they had to unpack their gun. And before they had it mounted Shard was away. If they had charged things might have been different. When they saw the Desperate Lark under way again the Arabs came on to within three hundred yards and there they mounted two guns. Shard watched them along his stern gun but would not fire. They were six hundred yards away before the Arabs could fire and then they fired too soon and both guns missed. And Shard and his merry men saw clear water only ten fathoms ahead. Then Shard loaded his gun with canister instead of shot and at the same moment the Arabs charged on their camels; they came galloping down through the forest waving long lances. Shard left the steering to Smerdrak and stood by the stern gun, the Arabs were within fifty yards and still

Shard did not fire; he had most of his men in the stern with muskets beside him. Those lances carried on camels were altogether different from swords in the hands of horsemen, they could reach the men on deck. The men could see the horrible barbs on the lance-heads, they were almost at their faces when Shard fired, and at the same moment the Desperate Lark with her dry and sun-cracked keel in air on the high bank of the Niger fell forward like a diver. The gun went off through the tree-tops, a wave came over the bows and swept the stern, the Desperate Lark wriggled and righted herself, she was back in her element.

The merry men looked at the wet decks and at their dripping clothes. "Water," they said almost wonderingly.

The Arabs followed a little way through the forest but when they saw that they had to face a broadside instead of one stern gun and perceived that a ship afloat is less vulnerable to cavalry even than when on shore, they abandoned ideas of revenge, and comforted themselves with a text out of their sacred book which tells how in other days and other places our enemies shall suffer even as we desire.

For a thousand miles with the flow of the Niger and the help of occasional winds, the Desperate Lark moved seawards. At first he sweeps East a little and then Southwards, till you come to Akassa and the open sea.

I will not tell you how they caught fish and ducks, raided a village here and there and at last came to Akassa, for I have said much already of Captain Shard. Imagine them drawing nearer and nearer the sea, bad men all, and yet with a feeling for something where we feel for our king, our country or our home, a feeling for something that burned in them not less ardently than our feelings in us, and that something the sea. Imagine them nearing it till sea birds appeared and they fancied they felt sea breezes and all sang songs again that they had not sung for weeks. Imagine them heaving at last on the salt Atlantic again.

I have said much already of Captain Shard and I fear lest I shall weary you, O my reader, if I tell you any more of so bad a man. I too at the top of a tower all alone am weary.

And yet it is right that such a tale should be told. A journey almost due South from near Algiers to Akassa in a ship that we should call no more than a yacht. Let it be a stimulus to younger men.

GUARANTEE TO THE READER

Since writing down for your benefit, O my reader, all this long tale that I have heard in the tavern by the sea I have travelled in Algeria and Tunisia as well as in the Desert. Much that I saw in those countries seems to throw doubt on the tale that the sailor told me. To begin with the Desert does not come within hundreds of miles of the coast and there are more mountains to cross than you would suppose, the Atlas mountains in particular. It is just possible Shard might have got through by El Cantara, following the camel road which is many centuries old; or he may have gone by Algiers and Bou Saada and through the mountain pass El Finita Dem, though that is a bad enough way for camels to go (let alone bullocks with a ship) for which reason the Arabs call it Finita Dem — the Path of Blood.

I should not have ventured to give this story the publicity of print had the sailor been sober when he told it, for fear that he should have deceived you, O my reader; but this was never the case with him as I took good care to ensure: "in vino veritas" is a sound old proverb, and I never had cause to doubt his word unless that proverb lies.

If it should prove that he has deceived me, let it pass; but if he has been the means of deceiving you there are little things about him that I know, the common gossip of that ancient tavern whose leaded bottle-glass windows watch the sea, which I will tell at once to every judge of my acquaintance, and it will be a pretty race to see which of them will hang him.

Meanwhile, O my reader, believe the story, resting assured that if you are taken in the story shall be a matter for the hangman.

After the Fire

When that happened which had been so long in happening and the world hit a black, uncharted star, certain tremendous creatures out of some other world came peering among the cinders to see if there were anything there that it were worthwhile to remember. They spoke of the great things that the world was known to have had; they mentioned the mammoth. And presently they saw man's temples, silent and windowless, staring like empty skulls.

"Some great thing has been here," one said, "in these huge places."

"It was the mammoth," said one.

"Something greater than he," said another.

And then they found that the greatest thing in the world had been the dreams of man.

The Assignation

Fame singing in the highways, and trifling as she sang, with sordid adventurers, passed the poet by.

And still the poet made for her little chaplets of song, to deck her forehead in the courts of Time: and still she wore instead the worthless garlands, that boisterous citizens flung to her in the ways, made out of perishable things.

And after awhile whenever these garlands died the poet came to her with his chaplets of song; and still she laughed at him and wore the worthless wreaths, though they always died at evening.

And one day in his bitterness the poet rebuked her, and said to her: "Lovely Fame, even in the highways and the byways you have not foreborne to laugh and shout and jest with worthless men, and I have toiled for you and dreamed of you and you mock me and pass me by."

And Fame turned her back on him and walked away, but in departing she looked over her shoulder and smiled at him as she had not smiled before, and, almost speaking in a whisper, said:

"I will meet you in the graveyard at the back of the Workhouse in a hundred years."

Preface to The Last Book of Wonder

Ebrington Barracks August 16th 1916

I do not know where I may be when this preface is read. As I write it in August 1916, I am at Ebrington Barracks, Londonderry, recovering from a slight wound. But it does not greatly matter where I am; my dreams are here before you amongst the following pages; and writing in a day when life is cheap, dreams seem to me all the dearer, the only things that survive.

Just now the civilization of Europe seems almost to have ceased, and nothing seems to grow in her torn fields but death, yet this is only for a while and dreams will come back again and bloom as of old, all the more radiantly for this terrible ploughing, as the flowers will bloom again where the trenches are and the primroses shelter in shell-holes for many seasons, when weeping Liberty has come home to Flanders.

To some of you in America this may seem an unnecessary and wasteful quarrel, as other people's quarrels often are; but it comes to this that though we are all killed there will be songs again, but if we were to submit and so survive there could be neither songs nor dreams, nor any joyous free things any more.

And do not regret the lives that are wasted amongst us, or the work that the dead would have done, for war is no accident that man's care could have averted, but is as natural, though not as regular, as the tides; as well regret the things that the tide has washed away, which destroys and cleanses and crumbles, and sparest the minutest shells.

And now I will write nothing further about our war, but offer you these books of dreams from Europe as one throws things of value, if only to oneself, at the last moment out of a burning house.

Dunsany.

Lord Dunsany, Edward John Moreton Drax Plunkett, the 18th Baron Dunsany, was born in London on July 24,1878. He was educated at Eaton and Sandhurst, and succeeded to the title in 1899. He served in the Second Boer War with the Coldstream Guards, and then settled at Dunsany Castle in County Meath, Ireland. In World War I, he was an officer of the Inniskilling Fusiliers, and by World War II, he was Byron Professor of English Literature in Athens. In addition to being a writer of short stories, novels, poetry, drama, and autobiography, he was also a big-game hunter and world-class chess player. Dunsany was quite well-known in his time: his stories appeared in *Collier's*, *The New Yorker*, and *The Atlantic Monthly*, and in 1916, five of Dunsany's plays ran simultaneously in New York. An author of more than fifty books, Lord Dunsany died October 25, 1957.

Manic D Press
Books

Next Stop: Troubletown. *Lloyd Dangle.* $10.95

Forty Ouncer. *Kurt Zapata.* $9.95

The Unsinkable Bambi Lake. *Bambi Lake with Alvin Orloff.* $11.95

Hell Soup. *Sparrow 13 LaughingWand.* $8.95

Revival: spoken word from Lollapalooza 94. *Edited by Juliette Torrez, Liz Belile, Mud Baron & Jennifer Joseph.* $12.95

The Ghastly Ones & Other Fiendish Frolics. *Richard Sala.* $9.95

The Underground Guide to San Francisco. *Jennifer Joseph, editor.* $10.95

King of the Roadkills. *Bucky Sinister.* $9.95

Alibi School. *Jeffrey McDaniel.* $8.95

Signs of Life: channel-surfing through '90s culture. *Edited by Jennifer Joseph & Lisa Taplin.* $12.95

Beyond Definition: new writing from gay & lesbian san francisco. *Edited by Marci Blackman & Trebor Healey.* $10.95

Love Like Rage. *Wendy-o Matik* $7.00

The Language of Birds. *Kimi Sugioka* $7.00

The Rise and Fall of Third Leg. *Jon Longhi* $9.95

Specimen Tank. *Buzz Callaway* $10.95

The Verdict Is In. *Edited by Kathi Georges & Jennifer Joseph* $9.95

Elegy for the Old Stud. *David West* $7.00

The Back of a Spoon. *Jack Hirschman* $7.00

Mobius Stripper. *Bana Witt* $8.95

Baroque Outhouse/The Decapitated Head of a Dog. *Randolph Nae* $7.00

Graveyard Golf and other stories. *Vampyre Mike Kassel* $7.95

Bricks and Anchors. *Jon Longhi* $8.00

The Devil Won't Let Me In. *Alice Olds-Ellingson* $7.95

Greatest Hits. *Edited by Jennifer Joseph* $7.00

Lizards Again. *David Jewell* $7.00

The Future Isn't What It Used To Be. *Jennifer Joseph* $7.00

Acts of Submission. *Joie Cook* $4.00

Zucchini and other stories. *Jon Longhi* $3.00

Standing In Line. *Jerry D. Miley* $3.00

Drugs. *Jennifer Joseph* $3.00

Bums Eat Shit and other poems. *Sparrow 13* $3.00

Into The Outer World. *David Jewell* $3.00

Solitary Traveler. *Michele C.* $3.00

Night Is Colder Than Autumn. *Jerry D. Miley* $3.00

Seven Dollar Shoes. *Sparrow 13 LaughingWand.* $3.00

Intertwine. *Jennifer Joseph.* $3.00

Now Hear This. *Lisa Radon.* $3.00

Bodies of Work. *Nancy Depper* $3.00

Corazon Del Barrio. *Jorge Argueta.* $4.00

Please add $2.00 to all orders
for postage and handling.

Manic D Press
Box 410804
San Francisco CA 94141 USA

manicd@sirius.com
http://www.well.com/user/manicd/

distributed to the trade
in the US & Canada by
Publishers Group West

in the UK & Europe by
Turnaround Distribution